Major Crush

How NOT to Spend Your Senior Year
BY CAMERON DOKEY

Royally Jacked
BY NIKI BURNHAM

Ripped at the Seams
BY NANCY KRULIK

Spin Control
BY NIKI BURNHAM

Cupidity
BY CAROLINE GOODE

South Beach Sizzle
BY SUZANNE WEYN AND DIANA GONZALEZ

She's Got the Beat
BY NANCY KRULIK

30 Guys in 30 Days
BY MICOL OSTOW

A Novel Idea
BY AIMEE FRIEDMAN

Scary Beautiful
BY NIKI BURNHAM

Getting to Third Date
BY KELLY McCLYMER

Dancing Queen
BY ERIN DOWNING

Major Crush

JENNIFER ECHOLS

Simon Pulse
New York London Toronto Sydney

SIMON PULSE
An imprint of Simon & Schuster Children's Publishing Division
1230 Avenue of the Americas, New York, NY 10020
Copyright © 2006 by Jennifer Stimson
All rights reserved, including the right of reproduction in whole or in part in any form.
SIMON PULSE and colophon are registered trademarks of Simon & Schuster, Inc.
Designed by Ann Zeak
The text of this book was set in Garamond 3.
Manufactured in the United States of America
First Simon Pulse edition August 2006
10 9 8 7 6 5 4 3
Library of Congress Control Number 2005933857
ISBN-13: 978-1-4169-1830-1
ISBN-10: 1-4169-1830-2

Heartfelt thanks to my editor, Michelle Nagler;
Katie McConnaughey; and everyone at Simon Pulse who
made my first taste of publication so delicious;

my wonderful agent and friend, Nephele Tempest;

my critique partners, Catherine Chant,
Elaine Margarett, and Victoria Dahl;

and the DH.

♥ ♥ ♥

This book is dedicated to my parents,
who have always supported my writing without question.

I must stress that they are *nothing like*
the parents in this book.

Except for my dad's profession,
and the notepads my mom used to write
my sick day excuses from school,
which were *all too real.*

Virginia Sauter is the first contestant in the competition for marching band fashion. Miss Sauter, a former Miss Junior East-Central Alabama, looks dapper in menswear. Her retro orthopedic shoes are from Dinkles Official Marching Footwear. Her drum major uniform trousers and coat are from Band Shoppe. And the faux diamond stud in her nose is from Jenna's Piercings Etc. in the Birmingham Mall. Let's give Miss Sauter a big round of applause!

One

I could keep my expressionless drum major face on while I strode under the bleachers and around the stadium to the bathroom. But then I was going to bawl.

Six thousand people, almost half the town, came to every home game of the high school football team. Tonight they crowded the stadium for the first game of the season. They had expected the band to be as good as usual. Instead, it had been the worst half-time show ever to shatter a hot September night. And I'd been in charge of it.

Me and the other drum major, Drew Morrow.

Allison knew exactly what I was doing.

She handed her batons to another majorette and hurried close behind me.

The band always took third quarter off. So I had about half an hour to get myself together, with Allison's help, before I had to be back in the stands to direct the band playing the fight song during fourth quarter.

I felt Allison's hand on my back, supporting me, as I stepped through the bathroom door. My eyes watered, my nose tickled, I was ready to let loose—

Unfortunately, about twenty girls from the band were in the bathroom ahead of me. Including Drew's girlfriend of the month, the Evil Twin.

You think it hurts your feelings that girls talk about you behind your back, until they tell you to your face. And they each wanted a turn. Every time, it started with "girlfriend" and ended with "bitch."

"Girlfriend, you think you're hot stuff, doctor's daughter. I like the nail through your nose, bitch."

"Girlfriend, you need to give it up. You call yourself the leader of the band. You only led us into sounding like crap, bitch."

Allison stepped in front of me, putting herself between me and them. She seemed

4

nine feet tall. She was a lot more threatening dressed in her majorette leotard than I was dressed like a boy. But she pulled at her earring with one hand, so I knew she was stressing out.

"You voted for Virginia," she reminded them.

"*I* didn't vote for her," called a clarinet.

"Well, *somebody* did."

"That's not what I heard," the Evil Twin said.

The Evil Twin was either Tracey or Cacey Reardon—I wasn't sure which one, and no one else seemed to know either. All we knew for sure was that the twins were evil. Or, one of them was evil and the other just looked the same.

I assumed the one currently dissing me was the one dating Drew. Because she sure seemed to have it in for me.

"What's that supposed to mean?" I demanded, walking forward to face her. I didn't understand what Drew saw in her besides heavy makeup, long hair, and enormous boobs. Maybe that was enough. "What do you mean, you heard nobody voted for me?"

"I mean, Mr. O'Toole quit his job in an

awful big hurry, and right at the beginning of school. Maybe he had to leave because you *convinced* him to count the votes in your favor, if you know what I mean."

My jaw dropped at the twin and her bad blue eyeliner. I couldn't quite get my brain around what she was saying. She wasn't *really* accusing me of having sex with the band director, was she? *So* ridiculous. I was the world's least sexy sixteen-year-old. I mean, there's a reason my parents named me Virginia.

"That's disgusting," Allison said to the twin. "Only a whore like you would think that up." Allison really was disgusted, or she wouldn't have talked that way. Usually she was above using words like "whore," calling people names, starting catfights in the bathroom—

"And *you*," the twin said to Allison. "Your daddy must have *bought* your votes for majorette. I know Mr. O'Toole didn't want any of *that*."

I wasn't sure the twin meant this as a racist comment. But that's the way the African-American girls in the bathroom took it, and maybe they knew best. Previously they'd wanted to stuff me down the sink. Now they came at the twin to flush her down the toilet.

I took the opportunity to pull Allison toward the door. I could cry later.

Before we managed to leave, the twin turned back to Allison and made the mistake of touching her majorette tiara.

Allison whirled around with her claws out.

"Fight!" someone squealed. Several freshmen made it out the door, still shrieking.

I hadn't witnessed a fight like this since a couple of girls got into it over a Ping-Pong game in seventh grade PE. And I was about to be the costar.

"Hey!" Drew boomed in his drum major command voice. His tall frame filled the doorway.

Allison and the twin stopped. There was complete silence for two seconds at the shock of getting caught. Then everyone realized it was Drew, not a teacher, and screamed because there was a boy in the girls' bathroom.

Drew reached through the girls. I thought he was reaching for the twin to save her from herself. But his hand closed over *my* wrist. I stumbled after him as he dragged me out of the bathroom and through the line at the concession stand, to a corner behind a concrete pillar that held up the stadium.

He let go of my wrist. "What. Were. You. *Doing?*"

I was gazing way up at the world's most beautiful boy. Drew was a foot taller than me and had a golden tan, wavy black hair, and deep brown eyes fringed with dark, thick lashes. And these were almost the first words he'd spoken to me since the band voted us both drum majors last May.

"Your girlfriend started it. Why don't you talk to *her?*"

"My girlfriend isn't drum major."

"So?"

"So, it's bad enough that I have to be drum major with you. It's bad enough that the band sounded like crap tonight. But you are *not* going to get in fights with people in the band. We have the same position. If *you* stoop to that level, *I've* stooped to that level. I'm not going to let you make me look irresponsible."

I had already known this was the way he felt about me. He'd tried his best during summer band camp to act like I didn't exist. Except when he spoke low to the trombones and they muttered under their breath as I passed.

"You're not my boss." My voice rose. "You don't get to tell me what to do."

He leaned farther down toward me and hissed, "We are not going to yell at each other in public. Do you understand?"

"You are not going to get in my face and threaten me. Do *you* understand?"

"Good job, drum majors!" called some trumpets passing by. They gave us the thumbs-up and sarcastic smiles. "Teamwork—who needs it?"

Behind them, Allison waited for me against the wall, arms folded, tiara askew.

I turned my back on Drew. We weren't through with our discussion, but we weren't going to solve anything by trading insults. And I wanted to make sure all Allison's cubic zirconia were in place.

I was glad about the quasi-catfight. I was glad Drew had reprimanded me too. Now I was pissed with the band and with Drew, instead of mortified at myself for being such a bad drum major on my first try.

And it was nice to find out that Drew knew I existed, after all.

TWO

"I hate this town, I hate this town, I hate this town," Allison chanted for a few minutes after we sat down in the stands. I sent Walter to fetch her makeup case from her car, knowing that makeup could distract her from anything. She would feel better when she was back to looking like her usual self.

Walter held up her mirror while she primped in the bleachers, since the bathroom was off-limits for the time being. She looked perfect again, dolled up in her glittering majorette costume, hair sculpted and curled around her tiara, eyes smoky, maroon lipstick perfect. As if she hadn't been about to kick the Evil Twin's ass only five minutes before.

Walter offered to brave the concession stand for us. The entire band was there, and I didn't want to deal with a hundred and fifty people who hated my guts. Twenty girls and one drum major had been enough.

Walter galloped down the stairs, and Allison turned to me. "You look like death. Let me put some makeup on you for once."

I laughed. "I can't wear your makeup. I'd *really* look like death in your Rum Raisin lipstick."

Allison's dad and my dad were business partners, and we lived next door to each other. So even though she was a year older than me, we'd always been inseparable. That is, until I quit the beauty pageant circuit. We'd grown apart in the past couple of years. But I needed to be a good friend to her because I was her only good friend.

Everybody liked Allison, but nobody wanted to get close to her. She came from the richest African-American family in town. Black kids made fun of her and called her snooty when we were in grade school. On the other hand, her family was one of only three African-American families in the country club on the lake that catered mostly to wealthy families vacationing from Montgomery or

Birmingham. She didn't like to play tennis with me there because she thought people were looking at her funny.

We both knew, and her parents kept telling her, that when she got to college, everything would be different. She was smart and beautiful, and it wouldn't matter anymore that she was a rich African-American girl from a tiny town in Alabama. The only sad thing was that she wouldn't leave for college for another year. A year was a long, long time for her to tread water.

But Walter had escaped already. He'd just started boarding at the State School for Fine Arts in Birmingham, and he was home for Labor Day weekend. I was happy for him, because his home life wasn't great—he lived with his mother in a bus at a camp-ground. And because the State School for Fine Arts was one of the best high schools in Alabama.

I was also happy for me. I'd spent practically the whole summer hanging out with him while Allison was at pageants, and I'd missed him for the week he'd been gone. But it was also a relief, because I was pretty sure he liked me as more than a friend. Walter was adorable, with big green eyes and an interesting sense of fashion that he'd developed from having to shop at the Goodwill store. But he wasn't for me.

Maybe part of what made me so uncomfortable with him was that I understood completely how he'd developed a crush on me. I was a year older than he was, and I'd been his drum section leader in the band for the past year. He looked up to me. It was natural that he would have a crush on me.

Like I had one on Drew.

Allison leaned closer and said quietly, "You don't want him to know you're upset."

Then, like the dorks we were, we both turned around and looked at Drew, who sat with his dad at the top of the football stadium. Grouped on the rows between us and Drew, several trumpet players and saxophone players glared at me like they wanted to pitch me off the top railing. In fact, Drew and his dad probably would have been glad to help me over.

I felt a pang of jealousy. Drew was close to his dad. I could tell the conversation Drew and his dad were having at the moment wasn't pleasant, but at least they were having one. I hardly talked to my dad anymore.

"Foul!" Walter jeered at the game, startling me and making Allison jump on my other side. "Dom Perignon?" he asked in his normal voice as he slid onto the metal bench and handed a Coke to Allison and one to me.

I drained the Coke. The night was way too hot for a wool band uniform.

Walter watched me. "I put Drew's band shoes back in his truck, like we found them."

"Thanks." Drew made me mad playing Mr. Perfect all the time. I had thought it would make me feel better to hide his lovingly polished band shoes so he had to wear his Vans with his band uniform. It hadn't.

"So, what happened in the halftime show?" Walter asked. "It reminded me of the Alabama Symphony Orchestra, but not in a good way. You know, before they start playing together, when they're tuning up."

Allison nodded. "There's a point in the majorette routine when I'm supposed to throw the baton on one and turn on two. I looked up at Drew and thought, *Is he on one? No, two.* And then I looked over at you, and you were on, like, thirty-seven."

I just shook my head. I was afraid that if

I tried to talk about it right now, the pissed feeling would fade, the mortified feeling would come back, and I'd start bawling in front of the tuba players.

Walter slid his arm around my waist, and Allison draped her arm around my shoulders from the other side. I tried to feel better, not just sweatier. They were the two best possible friends.

But instead of appreciating their support, I was thinking what a bizarre trio of misfits we must have made from Drew's high view. Allison, looking as glamorous as possible in her majorette uniform. Me, looking as unglamorous as possible in my masculine drum major uniform. And Walter, a fifteen-year-old boy who'd finally made it out of the bus.

Someone slid onto the bench beside Walter. Oh no, Luther Washington or one of Drew's other smart-ass trombone friends coming to rub it in. Or worse, the Evil Twin. I peered around Walter.

It was the new band director, Mr. Rush. Before I'd seen him today, I'd hoped that getting a new band director might help my predicament as queen band geek. Mr. O'Toole, who'd been band director for as long as I could remember, had gotten us into this mess by deciding we'd have two drum majors this year.

Then, knowing he'd be leaving near the beginning of the school year anyway, he sleepwalked through summer band camp. He let Drew and me avoid working together. I couldn't imagine what the new band director would be like, but any change had to be for the better.

Or not. Mr. Rush didn't seem like he was in any position to change the status quo. He was fresh out of college and looked it, maybe twenty-two years old. He could have passed for even younger because he was only about five foot six, the height of sophomore boys like Walter who weren't fully grown. I mean, I was five two, and Drew was impressively tall. I thought that made a huge difference in how the band treated us. I wondered how Mr. Rush thought he could handle a hundred and fifty students.

I was about to find out.

"Amscray," Mr. Rush growled at Walter. Walter leaped up and crossed behind me to sit on Allison's other side.

Mr. Rush stared at me. Not the stare you

give someone when you're starting a serious conversation. Worse than this. A deep, dark stare, his eyes locking with mine.

He meant to intimidate me. He wanted me to look away. But I stared right back. It felt defiant, and I wondered whether I could get suspended for insubordination just for staring.

I guess I passed the test. Finally he relaxed and asked, "What's your name?"

"Virginia Sauter."

He nodded. "What's the other one's name?" He didn't specify "the other suck-o drum major," but I knew what he meant.

I shuddered. "Drew Morrow."

Walter leaned around Allison. "His friends call him General Patton."

Allison laughed.

Mr. Rush ignored them. He asked me, "What's with the punky look? You've got the only nose stud I've seen in this town."

"Would you believe she entered beauty pageants with me until two years ago?" Allison asked. Allison always rubbed this in.

"I developed an allergy to taffeta," I said.

"No, she didn't," Allison said. "On the first day of summer band camp in ninth grade, she walked by Drew in the trombone section.

17

The trombones called her JonBenét Ramsey, and it was all over. She quit the majorettes and went back to drums."

"Is that true?" Walter asked me.

"You think I was born with a stud in my nose?"

"And she stopped wearing shoes," Allison added.

Mr. Rush eyed my band shoes.

"Well, I'm wearing shoes *now,*" I said. "Of course I can't be out of uniform at a game."

"Of course not," Mr. Rush said, looking my uniform up and down with distaste.

"More people might get their noses pierced if I started a club," I said. "Would you like to be our faculty sponsor?"

"And an attitude to match the nose stud," Mr. Rush said. He leaned across me to point at Allison and Walter. "You, princess. And you, frog. Beat it."

They scattered, leaving Mr. Rush and me alone on the bench.

Mr. Rush explained, "You learn in teacher training classes not to challenge students in front of other students, because all you get is lip."

"Did they tell you not to make fun of

your students' appearance? I have every right to wear a stud in my nose."

He laughed shortly. "I doubt that would stand up in court. Not in Alabama."

"Then I'm moving to Oregon."

He cocked his head and looked at me quizzically. "Come off the defensive, would you? I happen to agree with you. I'm just figuring out what's going on here." He glanced over his shoulder at Drew and his father at the top of the stands. "What's up with you and Morrow?"

"He was drum major by himself last year," I said. "Everybody knew he'd be drum major again this year. But Clayton Porridge was trying out against him. I wanted to be drum major next year, after Drew graduated. I figured I'd better go ahead and try out, just for show, so Clayton wouldn't have anything on me."

I looked down into my cup of ice. "I never thought I'd make it this year. A girl has never been drum major. And we've never had two drum majors. Mr. O'Toole decided after the vote that we'd have two this year, the two with the most votes, and that was Drew and me. I don't know what he was thinking." I made a face. "Though

I'm pretty sure what Drew's thinking."

"So a girl's never been drum major," Mr. Rush repeated slowly. "And all the flutes and clarinets are girls, and all the trombones are boys. Gotta love a small town steeped in tradition. Who needs this diversity crap?"

It bothered me, too, or I wouldn't have tried out for drum major. But it made me mad that Mr. Rush would come here from the outside and attack my hometown. "Where did *you* grow up?" I asked.

"Big Pine."

"Oh, like that's any better. Big Pine is just as small and just as backward as this place. Plus, the paper mills make it smell like last week's Filet-O-Fish." Actually, my town was too isolated to have a McDonald's, and Big Pine had one, which weakened my argument. I had very limited personal experience with the Filet-O-Fish.

"I'm really liking this lip," he said.

I knew I'd better back off.

"Which one of you got the most votes?" he asked.

"Mr. O'Toole wouldn't tell us."

Allison had a theory, though. She thought I won, and Mr. O'Toole just didn't want me to be drum major by myself. I mean, he didn't even want to let a girl try out. My dad had to threaten to call the school board.

Drew had been a terrific drum major last year. He'd won all these awards. But Allison's theory was that the band thought he was stuck-up.

Before, when he was just a sophomore trombone, he cut up with the other trombones. They would let out a low "ooooooh, aaaaaah" whenever Mr. O'Toole or the previous drum major, one of Drew's older brothers, said anything profound. Drew was happy-go-lucky. Everyone loved him. Especially girls.

But as soon as he got drum major last year, he buttoned up. He hardly even laughed any more. Allison thought the band had gotten tired of it and voted him out. There was no way of knowing, when Mr. O'Toole wouldn't tell us who really won.

I went on, "Mr. O'Toole said that since we were both drum majors, it didn't matter who got more votes. He didn't want to generate bad blood between us." I smiled. "It worked."

Mr. Rush rubbed his temple like he had

a headache. "When's the last time you had a conversation with Morrow?"

"A conversation?"

"Yeah, you know. You talk, he talks, you communicate."

"We had an argument just now because he sicced his girlfriend on me in the bathroom. Is that progress?"

He closed his eyes and rubbed his temple harder. "How about before that?"

"Communicate. Probably . . ." I had to think about this. "Never."

"Then how have you functioned at all? Even on your sad, limited level?"

I shrugged. "Mr. O'Toole would tell me where to go on the field, and then he would tell Drew where to go."

"I'm going to tell you both where to go," Mr. Rush muttered. "You see me in my office before band practice when we come back to school on Tuesday. And I want you to spend the long weekend contemplating how the two of you reek."

"I know," I whispered.

"If you performed that way at a contest, you'd get embarrassingly low marks. So would the band, because the two of you have them so confused. And the drums!

Though I'm not sure the drums are your fault. I suspect they reek on their own merit."

He stood, looking down at me with a diabolical grin. "I'm so glad we've had this chat. To be fair, I'd give Morrow the same treatment, but it looks like someone's beat me to it."

I nodded. "His father and his two older brothers used to be drum majors."

"What? A legacy? The Morrow clan has drum major tied up like the Mafia?"

"It feels that way."

"I should have kept my job in Birmingham at Pizza Hut," Mr. Rush grumbled as he stomped away.

I had to agree with this. Despite myself, I looked up one more time at Drew high in the stands. He and his father sat side by side in the same position, leaning forward, elbows on knees. The only difference was that Drew hung his head. Now Mr. Morrow pointed to Drew's Vans.

I imagined Mr. Morrow lecturing Drew in a Tony Soprano voice. "I'm counting on you to uphold the family name. I want you to off the broad. *Capisce?*"

Three

"You *are* a good drum major," Walter said.
"I mean, I assume you *could* be. You haven't
had a chance. But there's no reason for you
not to be a good drum major. You're musically talented. You're responsible. And
besides, you look cute in your uniform
pants."

I rolled my eyes. He made this kind of
flirtatious comment more and more often
lately. It made me so uncomfortable that I
probably shouldn't have come over to the
bus today. But my dad had the day off and
was likely to organize some wretched family
activity if I was around. Allison was at a
pageant all weekend, as usual. And I needed
to talk.

I inched farther away from Walter on his bed, which he had cleared of difficult-looking books so we could sit down. Some of our friends referred to the bus as the Bookmobile because the walls were stacked like a library, giving Walter and his mother even less space to move around.

The bus was divided into two rooms. The back room was Walter's mom's bedroom. I don't know why she bothered. She was hardly ever home. In fact, in the entire past year that Walter and I had been close friends, I'd probably laid eyes on her twice.

She was working on a PhD in psychology at Auburn University. This sounded impressive, like maybe they would move into a real house soon. Until you found out that she'd been working on one psychology degree or another almost since Walter was born and his dad left. And *then* you heard that she partied with her friends and didn't always make it home from Auburn at night. You wondered why she didn't use some of this book-learning in psychology on *herself*. This was the one thing Walter and I couldn't talk about, besides my dad. And Walter's crush on me.

The front room of the bus was Walter's

room, the living room, and the kitchen combined. We sat on his bed because it doubled as the sofa. My old-fashioned mother had forbidden me to set foot in a boy's room or sit on a boy's bed. I had never checked with her to see how the rules changed when a boy lived in a bus. Normally I would just shrug her warnings off, because I knew what I was doing. And it was only Walter, after all.

The way he'd been acting lately, though, I was tempted to give him the trusty old "my mother won't let me go inside a boy's bus unchaperoned" excuse. I tried to ignore that he inched toward me as I inched away. At least I had my drumsticks in my lap. I could jab him if he inched an inch too far.

"I'm starting to think it has nothing to do with being musically talented or actually directing the band," I said. "Drew can direct the band, and I can direct the band. But what Drew can do that I *can't* do is yell at people and make them jump. These girls in the bathroom reacted to me like I was one of them, or *below* them, even. They reacted to Drew like he was in charge. *I'm* supposed to be in charge too. What's the matter with *me?*"

Walter frowned at me and stared with his big green eyes like he was really considering this question. While I waited for the big revelation, I noticed that his eyes exactly matched the green leaves in the trees out the bus window behind him. He really was cute. I could totally see how I would be head over heels in love with him, if I were fourteen years old instead of sixteen.

I started tapping out a nervous rhythm on my knee with my drumsticks. I used to take my drumsticks with me everywhere because I wanted to practice constantly and be a better drummer. Now I took them with me because I felt naked without them.

Finally Walter said, "You're not a screamer."

I stopped tapping. "Oh, for the love of—"

"I'm serious. Drew hears a fight in the girls' bathroom and goes in to break it up. His first instinct is to yell. Well, let's say *you* heard a fight in the *boys'* bathroom, and *you* broke it up. What would you do naturally if you could solve it your way?"

"I would run in the other direction. You really expect me to go in the boys' bathroom? Let them kill each other."

"You know what I mean. Hypothetically."

I'd been thinking a lot about what Mr. Rush had said to me after he told Walter and Allison to beat it so he could talk to me alone. *Don't challenge students in front of other students, because all you get is lip.*

"I'd pull each person to the side and talk to them one-on-one about what was going on," I said. "I'd act like if they would please back off, I would consider it a favor. And I really would. I mean, I know everybody in band. Everybody in band is a friend of mine. Except for the Evil Twins, and anyone who happens to be calling me a bitch at the moment.

"For instance, Tonya, Paula, and Michelle were in the bathroom. I've had almost every class with them for years. And still they didn't stand up for me. Michelle brandished her flagpole at me like a Power Ranger. But they were caught up in the mob mentality and wanted blood. If Drew and Mr. Rush let me, I'd always talk to people on a personal level rather than yelling at them, because that's how I function."

"Then that's what you should do," Walter said. "You have to yell on the football field. But in rehearsal, you don't have to act like General Patton. Be yourself rather than trying to be a small, blond Drew, and you'll probably get better results."

This made sense, but it seemed too simple. "Can I do that? I've never heard of a drum major doing that."

"We've never had a girl drum major."

This took a few seconds to sink in. *Walter,* I said in awe.

"I know, I know," he said. "I know all about my own eye-hurting brilliance."

I waited for him to ruin it by suggesting some way I could *repay* him for his eye-hurting brilliance. That's what he usually would have done. But he didn't.

"Walter," I repeated, "you are so helpful. Except for the gross, horny, fifteen-year-old boy comments along the way."

"Hey. I am not gross."

"Thank you *so much,*" I kept gushing. "See, that's what I like so much about you. You're a boy, but it's like you're not. Talking serious with you is like talking to a girl."

I meant every word. But when I finished, I could tell from the look on his face that I should have edited my gushing.

"It's like I'm not a boy?"

I looked away from his angry green eyes and started tapping my drumsticks again. "You know what I mean."

His voice rose. "Talking to me is like talking to a *girl?*"

"That's a compliment," I said weakly.

"You can't say stuff like that to me."

Still tapping, I tried to act casual and blow it off. "Yes, I can. We've always been able to say anything to each other." Almost.

"Not anymore," he said. "Get off the bus."

I stopped tapping. "What?"

"You heard me."

I wanted to poke him with my drumstick, to tease him back into his usual good mood. But his green eyes were hard. I walked down what used to be the aisle, before the seats were removed to make room for stacks of books, and opened the folding bus door with the lever. I padded down the steps to the dirt outside and turned around to see if he'd changed his mind yet.

He closed the door behind me.

I walked along the side of the bus, standing on tiptoes to peer in. It was dark inside compared to the sunny day, and I couldn't see. But the bus wasn't air-conditioned, and all the windows were open to the breeze.

"Walter," I called. When he didn't answer, I rapped on the inside of a window frame with my drumstick.

"Stop," he yelled over the racket. "You're

being disrespectful of my home."

I stepped back and looked up at the bus doubtfully. Once upon a time, it had been a yellow school bus. But as Walter told the story, when he was twelve, he'd painted it brown in a futile attempt to make it look more like a house.

"When you remind me that you live in a sixty-room lakeside mansion," he exaggerated, "you're just making it harder on yourself."

I glanced through the trees at the sunlight glinting off the deep green water. "You live on the lake too, Walter."

"You know what I mean. I live in a bus in a campground on the lake. This is my mother's idea of permanent housing. I do not have my own private beach."

A squeak cut through the soft sound of wind in the trees as he opened the bus's emergency exit. He jumped to the ground with a towel draped over his shoulder. "Don't follow me," he said. "The public shower doesn't have a lock, and it's not fair. I couldn't follow you into your freaking boudoir." He walked down the hill toward the campground bathrooms, muttering about sixty-room houses and private beaches.

I wasn't naive. I understood there was a money difference that made people uncomfortable with me. It was always there between Walter and me, between me and almost any boy. For instance, today I wore ratty jeans and a faded T-shirt. Walter wore ratty jeans and a faded T-shirt. We looked like twins, or at least like brother and sister. But I paid full-price for my clothes at Abercrombie & Fitch in the Birmingham Mall, and Walter bought his at the thrift store.

But I wasn't going to let him get away with changing the subject. "Walter, if you're mad at something I said, okay. Let's talk about it."

He didn't even slow down. He kept stalking away from me under the trees.

"Walter, come on," I called. "You're going back to school tomorrow. I won't see you again for, what? Another two weeks?"

"If you're lucky," he yelled without turning around.

I wondered whether he meant I'd be lucky if he showed up again in two weeks, or I'd be lucky if he stayed away until then.

Four

On Tuesday I begged my English teacher to let me out of class ten minutes early. When she gave me the nod, I bolted out the door and down the stairs to the lunchroom.

Mr. Rush had told me to come to his office before band. That meant during my lunch period. Through long years on the pageant circuit, I was used to watching my weight, but I kept it down by jogging and by laying off the Doritos. I'd never skipped a meal in my life. And I didn't intend to start because of Drew Morrow. No matter *how* long his eyelashes were.

Seems Drew had the same idea. By the time I burst through the lunchroom doors, he already sat across the empty room, alone in the rows of tables and chairs, wolfing down a hamburger. He watched me as I dashed for the salad bar.

Usually I was picky, but today I grabbed a plate, piled it with lettuce, and spooned on whatever else was handy. I think this involved beets. I wasn't sure. It was red, whatever it was. I sat in the chair nearest the salad bar and shoveled it in without tasting it.

We faced each other across the rows, stuffing our faces, monitoring each other. There was no way I would let him beat me to that band room.

He made a move toward the doors like he was leaving, which made me start. You would think that if I was coordinated enough to walk down a pageant runway in high heels, or to direct the band, I could shove a fork in my mouth and stand up at the same time. Apparently not. I lost my balance, my chair scraped out from under me, and I landed on the floor.

Drew half-stood as if he were coming to help me up.

Too slow. I jerked up my backpack of books and ran for the door. A lunchroom lady blocked my way because I didn't take my plate to the dishwasher. Hurdling chairs, I raced back to my table, scooped up the plate, and made for the dishwasher. Drew was already there. He passed me, heading out.

I followed him as he sprinted down the hall. The bell rang, and the hall flooded with people. They blocked his way. They blocked my way too, but I was smaller. I ducked between them.

Then came a lucky break for me. The vocational ed teacher caught Drew by the arm and lectured him on running in the hall. *Shameful*, a responsible senior like himself. I blew right past them. I had a lead on him, but he would gain on me if we took the same route. I kicked off my flip-flops, stuffed them in my backpack, and took a shortcut outside the building.

"Ha," I puffed triumphantly as I sprinted barefoot through the cool grass. One for every step: "Ha ha ha ha ha!" I rounded the last corner of the building and heaved back on the heavy band room door. My eyes hadn't adjusted from the bright sunlight outside, but I dashed in the general direction of Mr. Rush's office. "Ha!" I shoved at the door.

The door said, "Ooof!"

The door gave way into the fluorescent-lit office, and I fell in with it. On top of Drew. Drew lay flat on his back on the floor, and I straddled him. We'd knocked sheets of music from a shelf as we fell. They fluttered down around us.

Mr. Rush peered over his desk at us. "Ah, Morrow and Sauter. Don't you knock?"

Without looking Drew in the eye, I backed off him and into one of the chairs in front of Mr. Rush's desk. I could have held out a hand to help Drew up, but I didn't.

Drew pulled himself into the other chair and dusted himself off, glaring at me.

Mr. Rush walked over, slammed the door, put his hand on my shoulder, and squeezed. "The first thing I want to know is what happened to this guy O'Toole. They wouldn't tell me shit at the job interview."

Right then I decided that Mr. Rush was the coolest. It wasn't that he cussed. It was that he cussed in front of us and trusted us not to complain to our parents, like he thought we were adults. Plus, he was coming to us for information about another teacher. I tried to recover, and answer, and act like nothing strange had happened.

Drew beat me to it. "He got fired."

"He didn't get fired," I corrected Drew, feeling superior because my information was better. "He quit."

"He got fired," Drew repeated, "because he was sleeping with Virginia."

"What!" Mr. Rush exclaimed. He looked from Drew to me in outrage. "And I have my *hand* on your shoulder!" He jerked his hand off my shoulder. "And I have the *door* closed!" He stepped behind me to fling open the door. "That's the *first* thing they teach you in education classes," he muttered. "Never touch your students. Never close the door while you're in conference with your students. I've been on the job one weekend and already I'm in trouble!"

I'd never seen a teacher throw a fit before either, so normally this would have held my attention. But I was busy calculating the meaning of what Drew had said. So it wasn't just the Evil Twin making up stories about me. I wondered how far the story had traveled, and how long people had been repeating it.

Maybe I'd gotten over the initial shock when the twin first accused me in the bathroom of sleeping with Mr. O'Toole. It never occurred to me to get really alarmed, or even to defend myself. Anyone who knew me knew how ridiculous the idea was that I would trade my virginity for drum major votes.

Besides, my parents had put the fear of God in me. Or anyway, the fear of sperm. My dad and Allison's dad were ob-gyns. This meant that they were doctors who delivered babies and otherwise took care of women's—you know—parts.

This meant that after I was home sick from school, my mother would scribble an excuse for me on a pad printed with a cartoon uterus and the slogan of a menopause drug: "Just like the estrogen she used to make!"

It meant that boys asked me if they could be my father's apprentice.

It meant that dinner table conversation every night was about the fourteen-year-old girls who had come to the hospital that day to have their second babies, and the evils of teen pregnancy. Sometimes I wished my dad worked at the cotton mill like everybody else.

Finally I turned to Drew and said, "It's *irresponsible* of you to start a rumor like that."

Score one for me. I was right on target with his responsibility fetish. He looked like I'd slapped him. Then he recovered enough to say—to Mr. Rush, not me—"It's not a rumor. She did—"

"Of course I didn't," I interrupted him calmly. "Mr. O'Toole is eighty years old."

"He's more like forty-five," Drew corrected me, as if this were going to sway the jury.

Sitting down at his desk, Mr. Rush held up one hand for silence. "I don't know what you've been up to," he said to me. He turned to Drew. "But I know you're acting like a jackass. If the rumor isn't true, you're irresponsible for spreading it. And if it *is* true, what do you think you're doing? *Tattling* on her for having sex with a teacher?" He looked through some papers.

I felt redeemed. And then, the more I thought about it, not.

Drew took a deep breath. "Excuse me, but did you say—"

"Jackass," Mr. Rush repeated without looking up. "Let's start again. What happened to O'Toole?"

"He quit," I said. "He'd been waiting for a position as a mail carrier for three years, and it finally came through last week."

"See," Drew said, pointing at me. "How does she *know* that?"

"Because I *asked* him," I said.

Mr. Rush made a show of stacking his papers, turning them and stacking them on another side, and placing them just so on his desk. "Let me tell you what *I* know. I'm living in a town that's so small and remote, it doesn't have a McDonald's. I've taken a job that's so bad, the guy before me was dying to break out and start his stellar career as a mailman."

His calm voice rose. "I have seventh graders for breakfast, eighth graders for brunch. For lunch, I have a class of a hundred and fifty teenagers and no assistant. And the two people I was counting on to *help* me are petty and immature"—he was looking at me; he turned to Drew—"and irresponsible!" He held up his hands on either side of his head and wiggled his fingers, like he knew irresponsibility was a scary monster for Drew.

Now he rubbed his temple like he did while talking to me Friday night, as if we were giving him a headache. "Kids, I'm going to have to insist that you cut the crap and help me out. I can't do this job by myself. I may have had a little argument with the football coach at the faculty meeting on Friday."

"Wasn't that your first day?" Drew asked.

Mr. Rush winced. "Okay, but that guy is an ass. He may have told me that the band needs to stop trampling 'his' football field"—he moved his fingers in quotation marks—"because it's turning the grass brown. I may have told him where to go. I found out after the meeting that the football coach is quite close with the principal.

"My contract runs out next summer. I need some leverage when it comes time to renew, or it's back to Pizza Hut for me. And tempting as that sounds right now, I have student loans to pay off." He shuffled through papers again and looked at some notes. "The two of you got the most votes in this drum major election, but there was a third candidate, right?"

"Clayton Porridge," Drew and I said together.

"Great. The two of you start getting along. You're dividing the band like East

Coast–West Coast, Tupac and Notorious B.I.G. Clean up your act. Make nice with each other. Make sure the band gets high marks at the contest in three weeks, or I'll fire both of you and make Clayton Porridge drum major. Got it?"

This couldn't be. I ventured, "Have you *seen* Clayton Porridge?"

"Plays trumpet?" Mr. Rush asked. "Looks like he eats paste?"

You can't do that, I thought. All the work I'd put into trying out. All the plans I had. I'd wanted to be the first girl drum major, wanted it worse than anything, for so long. But of course Mr. Rush could do whatever he wanted, because he was the band director.

Now I didn't think he was the coolest anymore. I thought something else entirely.

"You can't do that," Drew said.

"You're going to college, right?" Mr. Rush asked.

"God willing," Drew said drily.

"Need a teacher recommendation? I can give you one. Play nice with Sauter, and you know what it will say? 'Works well with others.' Don't play nice with Sauter, and it will say 'Fired.'"

"I have another idea," Drew said, taking charge again. "Last year I was drum major by myself. We went to three contests. I made high marks at all three, and I won best drum major at two of them. The band did great too. And Virginia"—he gestured to me without looking at me, like I was one of the filing cabinets lining the walls—"was the section leader of the drums when she was only a sophomore. The drums are so bad now because she and Walter left."

"Who's Walter?" Mr. Rush demanded.

"The frog from Friday night," I told him.

"Virginia's boyfriend," Drew said.

"He's not my boyfriend," I said.

Drew finished, "So why don't we just go back to doing what we did last year, which worked?"

Mr. Rush stared at Drew. It was the *I dare you* stare he'd given me Friday night. Drew shifted uncomfortably in his chair. Part of me wanted him to hold the stare. Part of me wanted him to look away.

He didn't look away.

Finally Mr. Rush said, "I bet you'd like that, wouldn't you, Morrow? No dice. But I do agree that Sauter should work with the drums. That would help the sound of the whole band. And it's not my forte. I flunked percussion in college."

"How did you graduate?" I asked.

"It's called a grade point average," he said self-righteously. "An F in percussion is canceled out by an A-plus in oboe."

I nodded. "So now I'm assistant drum major."

"No."

"I'm percussion drum major."

"No. We're making the best use of your talents." He turned to Drew. "Is she always this suspicious?"

"I wouldn't know," Drew said.

I was relieved Mr. Rush didn't take Drew's advice and toss me out on my butt. But I worried about making nice with Drew. We'd been Tupac and Notorious B.I.G. all through band camp (and I hoped I was Tupac).

Mr. Rush drew a line through an item in his notes, then tapped his pen on the page. "Now, Sauter. Can you tell me why you made that particular choice of drum major uniform?"

I shrugged. "Because that's what Drew wears. That's what he wore last year."

"Drew is a boy," Mr. Rush pointed out.

"Well, I don't know about *that*," Drew said.

Mr. Rush rolled his eyes. "Spare me the manly macho crap, Morrow." He turned back to me. "Morrow is a 'man,'"—he moved his fingers in quotation marks again—"and you're a 'woman,' and you need to stop trying to look like a 'man.' Trade in your pants for a miniskirt. Find some of those knee-high boots."

I remembered what Walter had told me at the bus: *Be yourself rather than trying to be a small, blond Drew.* But the outfit Mr. Rush suggested wasn't exactly the look I was going for either. "You want me to wear a miniskirt and long boots?" I asked him incredulously. "If I wasn't a slut before, I'm going to look like one now."

"I have news for you, missy. Your friend the princess is strutting around the football field in a sequin-covered bathing suit."

"Virginia knows," Drew chimed in. "She was a majorette herself, for about two days."

"Oh, that's right," said Mr. Rush. "And you made some JonBenét Ramsey crack, Morrow, and she went off and got her nose pierced."

45

"What?" Drew looked at me in shock.

"That's not why I quit the majorettes," I told Drew. "I mean, that wasn't the only reason." I turned to Mr. Rush. "I'll probably get expelled for saying this, but you're a real—"

Drew slapped his hand over my mouth. "Don't fall for it," he told me, watching Mr. Rush. "Remember he's trying to get rid of us."

I stared wide-eyed at Drew. Besides trying to pull my arm off in the bathroom Friday night, it was the first time he'd ever touched me. This close, he was so foxy that he almost gave me the shivers. Clarinets swooned over Drew. But I made it a point not to swoon over anybody, ever. Especially not somebody who'd just accused me of prostituting myself to an eighty-year-old.

Then Drew realized what he'd done. He snatched his hand away.

Mr. Rush put his chin in his hand and gazed at us, looking bored. "Here's the thing, Sauter. You're a pretty girl." He turned to Drew. "Can I say that as her teacher, or is it sexual harassment?"

"You're on the line."

"Then you tell her," Mr. Rush said.

"Don't you think she's a pretty girl?"

Drew looked at me and seemed to be studying me. I could feel myself turning red. Finally he said, "She's mean."

"Me!" I squealed. "What about—"

Mr. Rush held up his hand for me to shut up. "But is she pretty?" he asked Drew again.

"I have a girlfriend," Drew said.

"I'm not asking you to take her to the *prom,*" Mr. Rush said, his voice rising again. "I'm asking you if you think she's *pretty.*"

"Yes," Drew exhaled, not looking at me. I was relieved to see that *he* was turning red too.

"Prettier than you?" Mr. Rush asked.

Drew laughed. "Definitely."

"And after Friday night's debacle, don't you think we should use any means available to interest the audience and improve morale in the band?"

"Yes."

"And to that end, don't you think her uniform is inappropriate?"

Drew turned to me. "The trombones call you Mini-Me."

I said, "The trombones can shove it up their—"

Mr. Rush held up his hand for me to hush again. He repeated, "Get some boots and a skirt. Short. But not too short, do you understand me? I don't want to get arrested. Can you do that by Friday?"

I nodded. I would put my mom on the case. She could order something from a band uniform store online and have it overnighted. She'd be thrilled for me to show some leg again.

Drew asked, "While you're at it, can you make her wear shoes during band practice?"

"I think it's cute that she doesn't wear shoes," Mr. Rush said. "Oh, my God, did I just say that?" Shaking his head, he drew another line through his notes.

Next item. "And what's with your military salute at the beginning of the show?" he demanded. "This ain't the army. Spice it up a little." He pointed at Drew. "Dip her, like in the tango. Work on that in practice today while I try to undo whatever damage you've done to my marching band."

Drew closed his eyes. "I don't dance." He sounded very tired.

"You don't have to dance," Mr. Rush said. "Just do this one move. Sex sells. Throw the audience a bone."

Drew opened his eyes and folded his arms. "I don't think I can do that."

Mr. Rush said, "Sauter, do me a favor, would you? Lean out the door and ask Clayton Porridge to come in here."

"All *right*!" Drew bent down and banged his head on Mr. Rush's desk. Voice hollow against the metal, he said, "This was so much easier last year."

Five

When Mr. Rush finally let us go, I jumped out the door of his office and ran to tell Allison the news that I had become a boots-wearing hussy of a drum major who seduced elderly men.

"Sauter," Drew called after me.

I didn't stop. The tile was cold on my bare feet.

I heard him speed up behind me. He caught up in two strides and touched my elbow once, lightly.

"Virginia," he said.

I stopped and looked up at him.

"Since we're supposed to be friends, ride up to the stadium in the truck with me. Please."

I glanced back toward Mr. Rush's office. He stood in the doorway with his hands on his hips, glowering at me, sending me a telepathic message: *Remember the Pizza Hut.*

"All right," I muttered.

Drew always parked his dad's farm truck in the band room driveway like he owned the place. Boys in the band had already dumped the daily load of hay bales and farm implements—scythes or whatever—out onto the grass.

A line of boys stretched from the truck through the band room and into the instrument storage room. They tossed drums and the biggest instrument cases all along the line to land in the truck bed so Drew could drive them up to the football stadium for practice. I stepped forward to join the brigade.

And promptly got hit in the chest with a bass drum. I nearly fell with it, which would have made three times in one hour, a record even for me.

"Girl in the line," a boy murmured. Another said in falsetto, "Mini-Me."

I managed to hand off the bass drum just in time to get crushed by a tuba case. This time I smacked onto the cold floor with the huge black case on top of me.

"Ooooooh, aaaaaah," said the line.

Drew didn't say it. But Drew and the other trombones had started the "ooooooh, aaaaaah" to make fun of one of Drew's brothers when he was drum major. It hurt like Drew was saying it to me.

Drew lifted the case off me with one hand and swung it by the handle back into the line. Then he helped me up. He cupped his hand to my ear and whispered, "I told you to ride with me in the truck. I didn't tell you to *load* the truck. That case was bigger than you are."

"You didn't *tell* me to do anything," I said, not bothering to keep it quiet. "You asked me nicely. When you start *telling* me to do things, that's when—"

He glared at me, reminding me that I was about to get us fired. I glanced over his shoulder at Mr. Rush, who lurked, arms folded.

"That's when I'll go wait in the truck," I said, forcing a smile.

I climbed up into the enormous cab and slammed the door. Allison passed by with the majorettes just then. She did a double take when she saw me in Drew's truck. I could tell she was asking the other majorettes to wait for her, and I rolled down the window.

"How'd it go?" she asked. But then she saw the look on my face, and she understood *exactly* how it went. "That bad?"

"Drew told Mr. Rush that I spread my legs for Mr. O'Toole so he'd make me drum major."

"Busy girl. You're getting a lot of that lately."

"I know it. Maybe someone's trying to tell me something. My nightly sexual escapades are catching up with me."

"Really," said a passing drummer in mock shock. Another put his hand up to his cheek, with his pinky and his thumb stuck out, and mouthed, "Call me."

I watched them walk up the hill toward the stadium. "Oh, and Mr. Rush doesn't like my uniform. He wants me to dress like a trapeze artist."

Allison was not the logical person to complain to about strange outfits. She wore three-inch heels with her holey jeans. She always wore heels so she would be used to wearing them and wouldn't look uncomfortable in them onstage at pageants.

Drew slid into the driver's seat of the

truck and called across me, "Hello, Allison." They were both seniors and had all the AP classes together.

"Hello, Flying Frogini," she said.

Drew looked perplexed. He looked cute when perplexed. A cute, perplexed ass. "Pardon?"

"Mr. Rush wants me to dress like a trapeze artist," I explained.

He pursed his lips to hold in a laugh. "I was going to say. I've been called a lot of names since Friday night, but that's a new one on me."

"Well," Allison said through a tight pageant smile. "I guess I'll leave you two alone in Drew's truck. Against my better judgment." She went back to the majorettes, and I rolled up my window.

I could hear the noise of the band clustered in the driveway. They flirted with one another or warmed up on their saxophones. But the closed doors and windows of the truck muffled the sound. It was almost like Drew and I were alone together, for the first time ever.

Except that a *thunk* shook the truck every time an instrument case landed in the bed.

"I guess we should make a pact to be nice to each other," he said. "Or pretend to."

Thunk.

"The only pact I want to make with you is that we don't compete with each other at meals," I said. "I have no idea what I ate for lunch."

Thunk.

He felt under the driver's seat and handed me a crumpled bag of peanuts. Then he found a bottle of water for me and one for himself. "I'm trying to be nice to you," he said.

Thunk.

I swallowed an enormous handful of peanuts and washed it down with a big swig of water. "Being nice to me for five minutes does not make up for pretending I didn't exist all through band camp. Or for telling the new band director that I screwed the old band director. Is that rumor really going around the band?" I doubted this. Allison would have heard it and told me.

"Not around the whole band. Around the trombones. I think my girlfriend may have started it."

"I never would have suspected," I muttered. "Do you realize how irresponsible it was of you to even mention it to Mr. Rush?"

Drew gaped when I said the *I*-word, and he didn't even blink at the next *thunk*. "No one believes it, Virginia. It's a joke. Mr. Rush didn't believe me."

"What if he had? What if he'd told the principal? What if it had gotten back to Mr. O'Toole's wife? Did you think about that?"

Thunk.

"I was mad at you," he said softly. "I shouldn't have done it."

"The next time I'm mad at you, I'll tell everyone that you had sex with Mrs. Grackle down in home ec."

He put a hand to his mouth like I'd suggested some unspeakable horror.

Thunk.

"You see how it feels?" I asked. "No, never mind. I don't think you can. It's different for a girl. I'm in a position of authority, which was always a boy's position before this, and you want to make me into a cartoon. You want everyone to think that if I'm in charge, I must have slept with someone to get there.

"I couldn't possibly have been elected drum major by the people in the band. They couldn't possibly think I might do a good job. They couldn't possibly be tired of you

acting like you're too cool to talk to anybody, unless you're hanging out with the
trombones or picking which flute to date
this week."

Thunk.

"You have to act cool," he said. "Otherwise, people won't do what you tell them."

"*I* don't act that way, and they do what *I*
tell them. Sometimes."

"People expect something different from
you. You're a girl."

I'd gotten used to the *thunk,* but we
both jumped at the *knock-knock-knock-knock-
knock-knock.* Tracey or Cacey Reardon
rapped with her knuckles at ear level on
Drew's window. The shadow of evil
descended over the truck.

The Evil Twins had earned their name
through a long list of horrors. When they
were only four years old one or both of them
had tried to close their neighborhood play-
mates in the automatic garage door. In
middle school one or both of them had
peeled Craig Coley's fingers back until he fell
out of a tree and broke his arm. Nobody was
allowed to climb the big, tempting trees
at school after that. Just this summer one
or both of them had single-handedly (or

double-handedly) broken up three couples, including Elke Villa and Gator Smith, who'd dated forever. One or both of them probably would have done more damage if Drew hadn't picked this opportune time to decide that one or both of them were the girl(s) of his dreams.

That was just the stuff I'd heard about. They were a year older than me, in Drew's class. So until Friday night in the bathroom, I hadn't been privy to their day-to-day heinousness. Here was my second introduction. Drew cranked his window open, and she was screaming at him before the glass was all the way down.

"We're talking about drum major business," he told her calmly.

She explained, at a higher volume than necessary, that my presence in the farm truck bothered her. You would think he would ditch this loud parody of womanhood. Her eyebrows were overplucked, and her heavy blue eyeliner practically glowed. But sometimes boys liked that look. I guess.

"I'm giving her a ride to the stadium," he replied. "I'll see you up there." She still screeched, but he rolled up the window anyway, started the engine, and eased the truck out of the driveway and onto the road around the school.

Out the back window, I watched her watching us go. I knew she wasn't done with Drew—or me. "Can't you do something to shut that off?" I asked him.

"You're not supposed to yell at girls."

"Says who?"

"My dad."

Ah, Southern chivalry. Boys down here still pull out your chair for you and pick up your books if you drop them. The chivalry only goes so far, though. I've tested it. If you point out to them that your status as a female does not make you any less capable of opening a door all by yourself, they'll ask if you're PMSing. And hold the door open for you anyway.

The truck bashed over a curb and onto the grassy hill up to the stadium. The instrument cases, the peanuts, and I went airborne.

"Sorry," Drew murmured when we landed with a crash. "Look, I'm sorry for everything. I had no idea until the meeting with Mr. Rush—" He stopped and glanced over at me, then wisely turned forward again and steered the truck before we hit the stadium bleachers.

"I'm sorry for that JonBenét comment two years ago," he went on. "I remember thinking it was funny that you changed after that. But I never made the connection. We stand over there in the trombone section and basically foam at the mouth. We don't mean anything by it."

"That's not exactly how it went down. That's what Allison told Mr. Rush, and she may believe it. But you're flattering yourself if you think your opinion matters to me," I lied.

He stomped the brakes, and the truck spun to a halt in the dust. The rest of the band had hiked up the hill from the school. Boys jumped into the bed of the truck and slid the instrument cases out, or peered through the back window of the cab and put their lips to the glass.

"I have an idea for the dip Mr. Rush wants us to do," Drew said. "We can ask Barry Ekrivay to help us. He took ballroom dance lessons with his grandmother at the junior college."

I laughed. "You're kidding."

"I swear. We spent all last year giving him hell about it."

I thought it was a good idea. But I

wasn't going to tell Drew so. I took a long sip of water.

"I'm trying to be nice to you," he repeated. He gripped the steering wheel hard, looking away from me, barely controlling his temper. I could tell it was a good thing his daddy didn't let him yell at girls. "Wouldn't you rather suffer through being drum major with me than let Clayton Porridge have it all?"

The sliding noises in the bed stopped, and the dust settled around the truck. The majorettes paraded in front of us on their way to the field. Allison gave me a look that said *Hey, how's it going with the boy you have a crush on who happens to hate you?*

Behind the majorettes, both twins eyed me while talking behind their hands to their friends. I was definitely in trouble.

"Well?" Drew prompted.

"I'm waiting for you to come around the truck and open the door for me."

He rolled his eyes, cussed, and bailed out of the truck, slamming the door behind him. But by the time he reached the passenger side, he had a fake smile plastered to his face. He opened the door and extended his hand to help me out.

"Yes," I said as I stepped primly to the ground, the dust soft on my bare feet. "I'd rather be drum major with you than not be drum major at all. I'll pretend to be nice to you so I don't get fired. But don't expect me to be your friend."

Six

Drew caught Barry Ekrivay as he passed the truck, and talked quietly to him.

"You're going to do *what*?" Barry exclaimed.

Drew continued talking while Barry looked me up and down.

"The Evil Twin is going to be *so pissed* at you," Barry told Drew. "I shouldn't help you, anyway. You owe me an apology for an entire year of senior citizen jokes."

"I'm sorry," Drew said.

Barry still pouted. "The trombones better not send me a card on Grandparents Day again this year."

"Drew's sorry, Barry," I called. "We need your help. It's for the good of the band."

Barry looked up at me again. "Okay," he said so quickly that I was a little alarmed. Ever since school started last week, I'd had the feeling he was interested in me. Nothing big—I'd just caught him looking at me in band practice a few times when I wasn't directing. But I really couldn't tell. No one ever asked me out. And he certainly wasn't making nonstop sex jokes like Walter. I had shrugged it off as a figment of my imagination. Now I hoped he wasn't getting excited about being close to me as he helped us figure out this dance move.

Barry was good-looking, I guess. A couple of girls in my algebra class were into him. One of them actually *stole his first-place math tournament ribbon off the bulletin board and slept with it under her pillow.* This made me feel better about my own crush on Drew, and my sanity. And Walter's.

Personally, I didn't see what these girls saw in Barry. His clothes were too neat and his hair was too short. Very L. L. Bean. He was too wholesome for my taste. Which I suppose didn't say a whole lot for *me.*

We walked through the stadium gate and found a place off to the side where the stands hid us from the band on the field. Barry was starting to explain something to me about the dip when Mr. Rush burst through the gate, cussing to himself.

He stopped just long enough to holler at us, "Fred. Ginger. Out on the field. Play nice in full view."

Drew and I looked at each other. I mean, we shared a look. Us against Mr. Rush.

The zap of electricity that this look sent through me was devastating. Drew and I had *shared a look*. Now we were friends, or could be. Except that I'd just told him we couldn't be.

Still tingling with the power surge, I walked beside Drew and Barry through an opening in the bleachers and over to the end zone. The band was centered near the fifty-yard line, and Mr. Rush took them through some warm-up scales, but heads kept turning our way. Freshman flutes. Allison. Tracey/Cacey.

Drew leaned against the goalpost with his arms folded while Barry showed me the dip. "I'm going to put my hand here and my leg here," Barry told me.

I did not like his hand *there* or his leg *there*. I vowed to be the best dipee ever so he wouldn't have to show me this twice. "What do I do?"

"Just relax and let me do everything."

"That's not my usual styyyyle—"

I was hanging upside down, with Barry's face close to mine.

To avoid looking at Barry, I quickly turned to upside-down Drew. "I need a rose between my teeth, or some castanets. What do you think?"

"I think I should have gone out for football," Drew said.

"Try it. You'll like it," Barry said. Before I could inquire what exactly he meant by *that*, he pulled me up standing. He pulled too hard, then had to keep me from falling with a grip on my arm. "Whoops-a-daisy. You're a lot lighter than my grandma."

Drew walked over, shaking his head, and Barry explained what he should do. Boys can't lay a hand on each other unless it's violent, because they think they'll get cooties. So the explanation of the dip took a lot longer and was much more complicated than necessary. They talked about it in the abstract like it was an algebra problem. I was not at *all* sure that Drew got it.

While Barry watched, Drew came close to me and put his hand *there* and his leg *there*. "This feels so awkward," he said. He turned to Barry. "Are you sure?"

Barry twirled his finger in the air.

Drew flipped me backward and lost his hold on me. I landed square on the powdery white goal line. A smattering of applause drifted across the field from the band.

"Touchdown," Drew said. "You only need one foot in the end zone." He held out his hand.

As he hauled me up, I said, "That's the fourth time I've fallen on my butt today, and in some way you've caused all four."

He pretended to count on his fingers, which almost made me laugh. Then he started doing math in the air with an imaginary pencil, which *did* make me laugh.

Barry looked from Drew to me and back to Drew. "Are y'all getting along or not?"

"Of course," Drew said.

"Perfectly," I said, dusting my butt.

Drew and Barry started toward me.

"That's okay," I said. In a move that I never would have fathomed myself needing to do, I put up both hands to keep two senior boys from touching my butt.

In truth, I probably would have been able to stand Drew touching my butt. Barry, not so much.

"Let's try it again," Drew said.

"Great," I said. "We might as well try it with *me* on top."

Barry's eyes flew wide open. I realized what I'd said, and steeled myself for Drew's comment about liking it when the girl was on top.

Drew was not Walter. He just laughed. "I weigh a hundred and ninety pounds. But yeah, let's try it."

"I weigh one-ten. Let's not."

He put his hand *there* and his leg *there.* He flipped me backward even faster this time, and immediately lost his balance. But he didn't lose his hold on me. He fell with me. On top of me. Hard.

I couldn't breathe. Oh, God, I couldn't breathe.

He took his weight off me but hovered close over me. "Inhale," he said.

I held up five fingers.

"I know. I'm glad we're not going to the prom together."

Barry leaned over me. "You've killed her."

"She's tough," Drew said.

Mr. Rush's face appeared beside Barry's. "Are you okay?" he asked me with genuine concern.

I nodded and gasped, forcing air into my lungs painfully.

"I just knocked the wind out of her," Drew said.

Mr. Rush slapped Drew on the back of the head. "You pay attention, Morrow. There'll be hell to pay if you hurt my drum major. I'll have Clayton Porridge out in the middle of the football field, doing the cancan."

"The cancan is surprisingly difficult," Barry said. "It takes a lot more coordination than Clayton Porridge has."

Mr. Rush gave Barry the brain-melting stare.

Barry shrank. "I know this because I played Little League baseball with Clayton Porridge."

Mr. Rush kept staring.

"Sir," Barry added. He looked to Drew for help.

Drew rubbed the back of his head. "Thank you for your guidance, sir."

"Smart-ass," Mr. Rush said to Drew. He stalked away.

I croaked, "I don't like this game."

Drew held out his hand to me and hauled me up again. Across the field the band cheered like I was an injured football player who'd just recovered.

Barry stared at my hand in Drew's. It *did* seem like Drew held my hand longer than he had to before he dropped it. But then Barry said, "I know what the problem is. Drew, you're left-handed."

"So?"

"So, you need to turn everything around the other way, a mirror image of what you've been doing."

Without warning, Drew grabbed me.

"I said I don't want to play this gaaaaame," I said, but suddenly he had me leaning backward, just like Barry had. I wasn't about to fall down, and he wasn't about to fall on top of me.

His dark eyes were so close to me. I could almost feel his eyelashes brush my face as he blinked.

"That wasn't too painful," he said. And I did feel his breath on my cheek.

Oh, *wow*. I wished we could stay this way forever. Okay, he would probably get a cramp eventually. But I wished he would keep holding me, looking down into my eyes as if he really enjoyed touching me.

At the same time, in the back of my mind, I knew I should say something so he wouldn't think I'd been brain damaged in our fall. Finally I managed, "Easy for you to say. You didn't get the life crushed out of you by Notorious B.I.G."

He pulled me up and set me back on my feet. Then he whirled around, grabbed me, and dipped me again, like he was practicing getting his pistol out of his holster fast for a gunfight.

"Ooooooh, aaaaaah," floated across the field from the band.

"By George, I think you've got it," Barry said.

Drew ignored Barry at first. His dark eyes seemed to search my eyes for something.

Then he pulled me up to standing. "Thanks, Barry," he said. "I think we're good to try it on our own. Grandparents Day is right around the corner, and we'll get you something special."

I understood that Drew was dismissing Barry like he'd dismissed Mr. Rush. Barry did not seem to understand this.

Barry asked Drew, "So, what are you and the twin doing Saturday night?"

Drew dropped my hand. *Poof,* there went our romantic interlude. Thanks, Barry, my ass!

"I hadn't thought about it," Drew said. "I guess we might park in front of the furniture rental store and watch TV."

This seemed pretty uncreative of Drew. Sure, the movie theater had only two movies at a time to choose from instead of fourteen like the theaters in big cities, but we did *have* a movie theater. And there was always the bowling alley.

I tried to catch his eye to give him a questioning look. No luck. He stared off toward the press box at the top of the stadium. Which was weird in itself. Drew always looked people in the eye. It was part of his drum major intimidation routine.

It occurred to me that maybe he'd made up this date for my benefit. It was bad that he and the twin were going *parking*! It was good that they were parking in public, where down-and-dirty necking would be highly unlikely. Was he trying to tell me he wasn't serious about the twin, and there was hope for me?

Oh, good Lord. I was such a dork. He wasn't going to ask me out. He didn't like me that way. We weren't even friends. I'd made sure of that with my stupid comment when I got out of the truck.

"What about you, Virginia?" Barry asked without missing a beat, as if he hadn't even *heard* Drew, much less found his date plans bizarre. "What are you doing Saturday night?"

I was a half-second from blurting out the truth. Walter wasn't coming home for the weekend—and anyway, I figured he was still mad at me, because he hadn't called. Allison was competing in a pageant. So I planned a solo par-tay of practicing my drums, watching MTV, and then reading until two o'clock in the morning. When I relayed my schedule to Barry, I would edit out the part where I invented an excuse to drive into town for a few minutes and cruise by the Rent 2 Own store, checking for farm trucks.

I stopped myself just before blurting. If Drew was parking with the twin at the Rent 2 Own, I didn't want to let on that I was hanging out at home, alone. Anyone could guess this, but I didn't have to *admit* it.

Then I saw Drew's dark eyes detach themselves from the press box and focus on me. Then flick to Barry and back to me. And I knew my instincts had been right about Barry liking me. Barry was about to ask me out.

My mind went into overdrive. An excuse. Where was my excuse? I could use Allison as an alibi. But what if Barry had already found out casually from Allison that she didn't have plans with me? I knew the thing to do was be firm, stand my ground, and turn him down nicely. Otherwise he'd keep asking me out. But I didn't know how to do that.

Besides, Drew was standing there. I thought he might politely leave us alone for a minute. Then I could turn Barry down. Barry would still be mad, but at least I wouldn't embarrass the crap out of him and give the trombones something else to make fun of him about.

Drew said, "She's dating Walter Lloyd."

"You *are*?" Barry asked, eyes wide again.

I am? I thought.

"I didn't know that," Barry said. "I knew you were friends with him, but . . . Isn't he a year younger than you?"

I nodded.

Barry plucked his trombone from the grass. "Okay, then. Y'all have fun. Break a leg." He jogged across the field to the rest of the band.

Drew turned to me and smiled. "You're welcome. Now, let's practice the dip a few more times so I can really get the feel of you."

We stared at each other.

"That's not what I meant." He squeezed his eyes shut and sighed. "Every word out of my mouth this afternoon—"

"I know. Me too." I laughed so he wouldn't feel so self-conscious. Which was kind of hard to do, when I was more self-aware than I'd ever been in my life.

He opened those beautiful dark eyes and grinned at me. "You know what I mean."

Oh, yeah. "I know what you mean." I just wished he really meant it the other way.

He put his hand *there* and his leg *there*— gently this time. He dipped me slowly, with control. Holding me steady, he shifted his hands a little. If I didn't know better, I would have said he *did* enjoy touching me, after all.

"I'm not dating Walter," I breathed.

"I know you're not," he said, his lips

close to my lips. "I was just trying to get you out of dating Barry. That *is* what you wanted, isn't it?"

I struggled until he set me on my feet. "Then why'd you tell Mr. Rush in his office that I was dating Walter?"

"Oh. That was just to make you mad. You know, before we suddenly became chums." He nudged me on one shoulder with his fist, chumly. "You didn't want to go out with Barry, did you?"

"No," I said emphatically. "And I didn't want to hurt his feelings. But I also didn't want to lie to him. It seems underhanded."

Drew shrugged. "Then why didn't you say something?"

"I was too stunned by your rude interruption."

"Oh, come on." He put his hands on me and dipped me slowly, gently. "Barry only asked you out in front of me so you couldn't say no. He knew you wouldn't want to embarrass him. One underhanded trick deserves another."

"But it's going to get around the whole school that I'm dating Walter. What if I wanted to go out with someone else?" Too late I realized that I probably sounded like I wanted to go out with Drew.

Which I did.

"What if you did?" he asked evenly, holding my gaze with his dark eyes.

"Then he wouldn't ask me out now."

Drew smiled. "Maybe he would."

I wanted to know how this mythical boy could ask me out. Would he brick his girlfriend and her twin sister up in the instrument storage room like in 'The Cask of Amontillado'?

Maybe Drew was just flirting with me, pointlessly, for fun. Maybe he *did* like touching me during the dip, even though it didn't mean anything to him. That was cool. I could enjoy a football season of flirting with Drew and touching Drew. If I didn't die of heart palpitations.

Or heartbreak.

He set me up standing. "It was meant as a favor. Just take it as a favor and say, 'Thank you, Drew.'"

"Thank you, Drew. May I have another?"

"Drum majors," the band called across the field. It was time to run through the halftime show, and Mr. Rush was motioning us over. "Horrible drum majors," someone else called. "Hey, really bad drum majors."

The laughing look in Drew's eyes faded. *There* was the look I'd come to know and love, the one that said he wanted to pitch me off the top of the bleachers.

We walked back toward the band together. "So, why *did* you get your nose pierced?" he asked.

"I don't even discuss that with my *real* friends, much less my *fake* friends."

I thought that would shut him down, and we would just blend in with the rest of the band wandering to their starting positions for the show, and not talk to each other for the rest of practice.

No, he wasn't finished. "Aren't you afraid it will get infected?" he asked.

"My dad's a doctor. I have twenty-four-hour surveillance on my antibodies."

We'd almost reached the band. Allison was talking to Drew's best friend, Luther, and trying her best to look disinterested.

"Does it hurt?" Drew asked.

I wished I had a dime for every time someone had asked me that. Usually I told the truth: It hurt like hell when I had it done, but now I couldn't feel it. Like getting your ears pierced.

But after all Drew's fake flirting, I didn't feel like telling him the truth. I felt like embarrassing him, if I could. I gave it my best shot.

"Poor Drew," I said. "You're so innocent."

We'd walked close enough to the band that Luther heard this. He laughed really, really hard. Drew just stood there. Luther put his arm around Drew's shoulders. "Bro, we need to talk."

As Luther led Drew away, Drew gave me a sideways glance. He didn't look mad at me anymore. Dark eyes darker, long lashes heavy. He looked . . . I wasn't sure *what* that look was.

But he wasn't mad.

I watched him duck with Luther past the flags. Then I turned to Allison. "Luther's cute," I said hopefully. He was in her AP classes, like Drew. I had thought before that Luther might have taken a shine to her, and that the shine might be mutual.

Well, maybe not. Allison tossed her head. "He dresses like the 'hood."

"That's ridiculous. You're such a snob. He dresses cool. And our town isn't big enough to have a 'hood."

She sniffed. "So, did Drew ask you out yet?"

"No, Barry asked me out. Drew just went down on me. Did you see it?"

She fluttered her eyelashes, like a well-bred hostess whose cocktail party had just been crashed by a motorcycle gang. "For a virgin, you have the dirtiest mind."

"You're one to talk, Rapunzel. Let down your hair." I poked one of her gelled finger waves.

She removed my hand with two manicured fingers. "Are you kidding? It took me hours to get it this way." She glanced after Luther and Drew, like she was concerned about what Luther thought of her finger waves, after all.

Then she said, "Speaking of hairdos. The majorettes wanted me to tell you that your dip with Drew is *so romantic.*"

I shouted laughter, and the nearby saxophones turned to stare at me. "Y'all are real bored over there," I said.

"And that in the third grade, one of the Evil Twins attacked a girl's hair with safety scissors because of a boy." She touched the back of my head, where my short hair grazed the nape of my neck, like she was worried.

Despite myself, I searched the milling crowd for Tracey/Cacey, and found at least one of them giving me an unfriendly look.

I said, "I'll keep that in mind."

Seven

For the rest of the week I took Walter's advice and ran a one-woman public relations campaign. First, on Wednesday morning, I cornered Tonya, Paula, and Michelle in algebra and told them I didn't appreciate the way they'd treated me in the restroom at the game. Now that they were away from the mob, they said they were sorry. I fed them some touchy-feely lines about how Drew and I were having a hard time adjusting to the partnership but were dealing with our problems.

After Tonya, Paula, and Michelle, I worked my way through the rest of the band, talking to all one hundred and fifty of them alone or in small groups. All of them, that is, except Drew's senior trombone friends. And the Evil Twins.

People actually were nice to me about it and at least pretended to understand and cooperate. By practice on Friday, I could feel a change in the atmosphere, like the pressure had dropped.

Or the reason for the weather change could have been that the band sounded so much better with a solid rhythm section underneath it. I'd worked hard with the drums all week. They finally sounded like they were playing their parts rather than dropping their drums and drumsticks from a ten-story building.

Friday after school four buses parked in front of the band room. The band was headed for the farthest football game of the year, down somewhere in southern Alabama. It would take forever to get there. We were only waiting for Mr. Rush to show up from his faculty meeting.

I was stuck chaperoning the freshman bus. I should have complained that I got the freshman bus and Drew got the senior bus. It made me look like assistant drum major. And I didn't look forward to the three-hour ride with screaming freshmen. That was a downside of being drum major—the *respon-sibility*. I'd claimed the front seat as a sort of escape hatch.

I sat on the stairs of the freshman bus, tapping my drumsticks on the rubber foot-pad of the stair. Drew sat with the twin on the wall next to the band room door.

I tried not to look at them, but it was only natural that I would glance in their direction every now and then. They were the only thing to look at against the expanse of concrete and grass. And I was there first.

Drew glanced over at me. *You dummy,* I thought. Of course the twin caught him looking at me, and she glared at me like I'd drawn his eye on purpose. Then they had a little chat. He glanced up at me again, uncomfortably. She glared at me.

Finally I got tired of the whole thing. I put my drumsticks down, put my knees up and my elbows on my knees and my chin on my fists, and just stared the hell out of them. I stared Drew up and down like he was something good to eat. I even licked my lips when he wasn't watching and the twin was.

Well, that was it. Now she *really* glared at me. We eyeballed each other like it was a game of eye-chicken. And it wouldn't be me who blinked first.

Drew passed a hand in front of her face like she was blind, and she blinked. Then he pushed her off the wall with a very inappropriate love pat to the derrière that was probably against school rules, and she scampered to the senior bus.

Mr. Rush was finally walking down the hill from the school. With him came Ms. Martineaux, the track coach, who was about his age and two inches taller. He said something to her and pointed her toward the senior bus. Then he motioned to me. I met him in the grass, along with Drew.

Mr. Rush rubbed his hands together. "The two of you are getting along great, right?"

Drew and I looked at each other uncomfortably. It wasn't the *us against Mr. Rush* look anymore.

"The show is coming along well for the contest, right?" Mr. Rush went on. "Because I may have gotten myself in some more trouble."

I asked, "Can't you just stop going to the faculty meetings?"

"This had to be done, Sauter. You know

how you have a white Miss Homecoming and a black Miss Victory every year? This violates desegregation laws. I can't believe no one's questioned it before."

"Probably because it's a holdover from forty years ago," Drew said, "when the black and white high schools were separate. The white high school had their Miss Homecoming, and the black high school had their Miss Victory. When they integrated, they kept both."

"Right," I said, nodding. "People get very, *very* touchy when you mess with their traditions."

Drew poked me once in the ribs. I might have flirted back with him, or at least stepped a little closer to him. Except that a poke in the ribs meant nothing next to a love pat to the derrière.

Mr. Rush continued like he hadn't noticed Drew touching me. "Separate but equal. Illegal. And I said so loudly enough in the faculty meeting that the tradition is no more. From now on, the girl who gets the most votes will be Miss Homecoming. And the runner-up will be Miss Victory. No matter what race they are."

I thought about how this would affect

Allison. She probably would be a candidate for Miss Homecoming/Miss Victory when the nominations were counted next week. She'd always been a maid on the homecoming float. She expected to be Miss Victory. Probably everything would stay the same under Mr. Rush's new rules.

Mr. Rush still ranted. "You can't designate school positions by race. I don't care what the tradition is. And I don't care what the principal thinks of me for saying so."

Drew and I looked at each other again.

"Okay, that last part is bullshit," Mr. Rush admitted.

Drew gestured toward the senior bus. "What's Ms. Martineaux here for? Your bodyguard after the faculty meeting?"

"I almost forgot to tell you," said Mr. Rush. "Morrow, you and Sauter will be in charge of the freshman bus."

I hadn't wanted the freshmen, but now that part of my responsibility was being taken away, I wanted it back. I didn't need Drew's help. I said, "The bus is packed. There's not enough room for Drew to have a seat."

"Share a seat," Mr. Rush said. "In fact, share the backseat. Lord knows we don't want kids feeling each other up back there."

I felt myself flash red at the idea. I must have looked like a traffic light every time I got around Drew and Mr. Rush started in with his comments.

Worse, Drew didn't hide that he hated this idea. "I'm supposed to be on the senior bus."

"Right, with your squeeze," Mr. Rush said. He reached up to grip Drew's shoulder sympathetically.

"Squeezes," I corrected him.

Mr. Rush laughed. "Good one." He gripped Drew so hard that Drew winced. "You're out of luck, Morrow. The flag coach is chaperoning the sophomores, I've got the juniors, and Ms. Martineaux has the seniors. We need to break her in gradually. I don't expect seniors to throw each other out the window. Freshmen, I'm not so sure. It may take both of you to handle them."

"We don't need another chaperone," I said. "I can handle the freshmen fine."

"He's using this as an excuse to come on to Ms. Martineaux," Drew said.

Mr. Rush folded his arms and gave Drew the stare.

Drew folded *his* arms and stared right back.

This went on for a few seconds. Finally Mr. Rush said, "Try to foil me, Morrow. Cross me, and I'll cross you." Drew and I watched him walk to the junior bus.

I turned and looked up at Drew. "What was that? Some secret guy code?"

"Yeah," Drew said without meeting my eyes. "I'd better get my uniform."

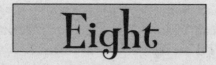

Eight

I climbed onto the freshman bus and announced that everyone on the left side had to move up one seat. This was the equivalent of throwing a hurricane onto the bus, but it seemed more fair than telling the people in the backseat that they had to move to the front. People fought for the backseat like it was a backstage pass to a Maroon 5 concert.

The couple in the back didn't appreciate my kindness at all. They wouldn't budge. I tried to explain the situation in terms they could understand: Mr. Rush was crazy.

Drew climbed onto the bus and walked down the aisle behind me, towering over the freshmen. He said to the couple,

"Move." They scrambled into the next seat. He dropped his uniform bag on the floor and slid next to the window.

Drew was the real drum major, and I was someone to be ignored. But standing there in the aisle with my hands on my hips didn't do any good. The bus was starting. And Drew couldn't even see me being mad, with his head leaned back on the seat and his eyes closed.

The bus lurched forward. I had to sit down next to him before I fell. "What's your problem?" I asked. "Did you get guff from the Evil Twin because you're not riding to the game with her?"

He opened his eyes and looked at me uneasily. "Could you hear her yelling all the way in here?"

I shook my head.

He closed his eyes again, took a deep breath, and let it out slowly through his nose. "It's kind of a relief not to have to deal with that for three hours."

Was he saying he'd rather be around me than the twin? Knowing the twin, this wasn't saying much. But he was dating her. He was saying I was better than his girl-friend. Right?

Seems like he *did* care what I thought of him, at least. He opened his eyes, sat up, and asked, "Are you mad at me?"

I batted my eyelashes at him. "Why in the world would I be mad at you, Drewkins?"

He pursed his lips to keep from laughing, an expression I was growing very fond of, unfortunately. "The way you were looking at me outside the bus before Mr. Rush came down."

"I was looking at you that way because your girlfriend was shooting daggers at me through her own eyeballs."

"She's not real into you. She thinks I like you."

Oh, *interesting*. "Why would she think that?"

"Because we're getting along now. And because of the dip. And sitting in the backseat of the bus together isn't going to help."

I wanted to ask, "Well, *do* you like me?" But of course I didn't. This was actually sort of somewhat halfway serious drum major business, for the good of the band and getting along and all that. I said, "It's your job to keep her off me. If you can't keep your girlfriend from talking ugly about me behind my back, you're not keeping up your end of the bargain for us to be friends."

"But that would be if we were *real* friends. I thought we were *fake* friends."

Maybe he was just making fun of me for what I'd told him about my nose stud last Tuesday. While I was still trying to work this out in my head, he asked, "Have you been talking to the band about what happened at the game on Friday?"

I wondered if he was angry that I'd run the public relations campaign behind his back. "Some," I said cautiously. "Why?"

"Because people have apologized to me for things they said to me last Friday night."

"See?" I grinned. "Aren't you glad you have me on your side?"

"If it weren't for you, there wouldn't be a problem." Almost as soon as the words left his lips, he followed quickly with, "I'm sorry, Virginia. It slipped out. I'm still a little touchy about the whole thing, okay? Virginia." He put a hand on my shoulder.

But I'd turned my back on him. If he was going to be an ass, I didn't care *how* long his eyelashes were.

He took his hand off my shoulder.

The foothills of the Appalachians around our town flattened into farmland on the hour's drive southwest to Montgomery. I knew from trips to the beach with my parents that from there, cotton fields, soybean fields, peanut fields, and cow pastures stretched all the way to the ocean. Of course, we weren't getting anywhere near the ocean this time. The game was in the middle of nowhere. As if our own town hadn't been nowhere enough already.

I spent the trip talking to Ariel James, a shy freshman who wanted to try out for drum major when I graduated. She was teaching herself to write music for band, but she played saxophone and needed help with the drum parts. I tapped rhythms for her with my drumsticks on the metal back of her seat.

This probably annoyed everyone else on the bus. I know it annoyed Barry's little sister, Juliet, who shared the seat with Ariel, because she kept telling me so.

I'd hoped it would annoy Drew. But the few times I stole a glance at him, he seemed absorbed in studying a book of SAT words. Which was strange. I'd never noticed Drew studying anything before. And I always noticed Drew.

As soon as the buses parked, he edged around me in the seat and left the bus without another word. I knew he had to help the boys unload the U-Haul of instruments. After he disappeared down the stairs, I dove for his uniform bag and pulled out his band shoes. Ariel and Juliet watched me. I put my finger to my lips.

"Virginia," Allison called from outside the bus, right on schedule.

I dropped Drew's shoes through the window to her, then leaned out. "Thanks," I said.

"No prob." She tucked the shoes into the back waistband of the sweatsuit she wore with her majorette boots and tiara, as if nobody would notice the large growth on her butt. "So, you really rode all the way down here in the make-out seat with Drew Morrow?"

"He talked my ear off the whole time. And the perv wouldn't keep his paws off me. I had to beat him away with my drumsticks. Be sure to tell his girlfriend the serial killer." I laughed at my own jokes. "And how was your trip? Did you suddenly bond with everyone on the bus and decide you want to spend the rest of your life in your hometown?"

"No, but it *does* look pretty good compared to this place." She nodded into the sunset at a barbed wire fence that ran along the back of the football stadium. Behind the fence was a herd of . . . I think llamas.

I was about to tell her about the Miss Homecoming/Miss Victory trouble that Mr. Rush had stirred up, when I heard a scuffle and a scream behind me on the bus. Time to break up a fight over an iPod, which was strictly prohibited on band trips. The iPod and the fight.

It quickly turned into trumpets versus tubas. I tried to talk them down soothingly. When that didn't work, I threatened them with laps around the football field during band practice on Monday. I couldn't tell them I'd tattle on them to Mr. Rush, because that would undermine my own authority.

Drew climbed back up the stairs. Just what I needed—Drew to save the day. His T-shirt stuck to his chest with sweat, and beads spilled from his hairline down his cheeks as he walked down the aisle. "Sit down," he said in passing.

Instantly the fight broke up, and everyone sat down in silence. The whole bus turned to watch Drew make his way over uniform bags and around coolers in the aisle to our seat in the back.

I stood in the aisle, looking like an idiot. It didn't seem possible that a fight so big was over so quickly. There ought to be something left for me to take care of.

But Drew was in charge.

It was all I could do to keep from giving him a piece of my mind. But I didn't want to get fired. As I walked slowly toward him down the aisle, I recited to myself, *Pizza Hut, Pizza Hut.*

The silence shifted and then lifted around us as everyone unzipped their uniform bags and started to change clothes. Without looking at Drew, I sat beside him and pulled my T-shirt halfway off over my head.

Nobody wanted to sit in their band uniform on the bus for three hours. It felt uncomfortable and looked dorky. But there wasn't anywhere to change except the bus. The trick was to wear something skimpy but decent under your clothes, like a bathing suit or a sports bra, so you could change on the bus while boys watched.

I hadn't really cared when I chose my tank top with a built-in bra, because I had thought

I would be stuck alone on the freshman bus. Now I suddenly cared very much what I looked like changing while a boy watched.

When I tugged the T-shirt the rest of the way off my face, Drew was sitting with his back to the bus windows, staring at me. Hard.

"Do you *mind*?" I asked.

"I just wanted to see what you got."

My heart stopped.

His dark eyes widened. "Your uniform! I wanted to see the uniform you got."

Rats.

I shrugged my uniform coat on over my tank top. I fastened my miniskirt over my shorts, then pulled my shorts out from underneath. I was wearing matching briefs like cheerleaders wore so the crowd wouldn't get an eyeful if my skirt flipped up. But I wasn't sure whether the briefs qualified as decent, like bathing suit bottoms, or indecent, like underwear. I figured I'd better not expose them to the freshmen and, uh . . .

Despite myself, I glanced at Drew. He was still staring at me, all right. And not at my face, either. Then his eyes slowly traveled up to meet mine.

I turned away to zip up my knee-high boots. Finally I leaned back in the seat and crossed my ankles on an ice chest in the aisle, as if I were cool. Which, I assure you, I was not. "Well?" I asked.

"Well," he said. And he pulled off his sweaty T-shirt.

My mouth dropped open. As he rummaged in his bag, I tried to find a good time to repeat snippily, "I just wanted to see what you got." But my brain wasn't working.

I'd expected him to be thin, with a farmer's tan ending just above his elbows. Instead, he had the strong, tanned body of a farm boy used to baling hay, or swinging scythes, or whatever it was farm boys did in modern times, with his shirt off.

Suddenly the seat was too small for the two of us. The entire bus was too small for Drew with his shirt off. In the seat across the aisle from us, Juliet pressed both hands to her mouth, and even Ariel gaped. Then a high, feminine "ooooooh, aaaaaah" broke out.

Drew looked around the bus confusedly, like, *Who, me?* He went back to his uniform bag, pulled on a clean T-shirt and his jacket, and continued to rummage. "Have you seen my shoes?"

"Don't tell me you lost them again."

He stopped. I could tell he was reviewing packing his bag. He was wondering whether he'd lost his mind.

"Just wear your Vans again," I said. "They're black all over, and they look like band shoes from a distance. I don't think Mr. Rush noticed you were wearing them last Friday."

"My dad noticed. My dad will kill me."

"Surely your dad isn't coming to the game. Even *my* sickeningly supportive parents didn't come. It's too far."

He stared down at his Vans. This was really tearing him up. I wondered if he could hear his dad in his head, using the *I-*word.

He shook his head like he was shaking his dad out of his hair with the sweat. "You ready?" he asked. I nodded and stood up. He followed close behind me down the aisle with his hand on my back, like we were a couple. He even pointed threateningly at a few boys who whistled when they saw me.

Mr. Rush was laughing up at Ms. Martineaux, who stood in the doorway of the senior bus. When we walked over, she disappeared back inside the bus, and Mr.

Rush turned to us. And turned to me. And raised his eyebrows.

"Is this uniform okay?" I asked.

"Tell her, Morrow."

Drew told me, "You look hot."

"What?" Mr. Rush whacked Drew on the chest. "That's not what I was going to say!"

Drew colored. "Then why couldn't you tell her yourself?"

"Uh-uh," said Mr. Rush. "No way. You're not pinning this on me. You got yourself into this one. And you already have girlfriends." He walked away cackling.

Nine

I should have known something was wrong with Drew when he didn't pay attention to the football game. He usually was one of those people who actually watched the game. I relied on him to signal me when our team had scored and we needed to play the fight song. Football couldn't hold my interest. I waved to my friends on the cheerleading squad or watched the llamas try to paw through the barbed wire fence at the edge of the end zone.

Above us in the stands the band yelled, "Drum major! We need a drum major!"

Our team had made a touchdown. Drew started like he'd been asleep, and we jumped up to direct the fight song.

The first time this happened, Mr. Rush didn't seem to notice because he was busy talking to Ms. Martineaux. The second time, he gave Drew and me the stare.

I *did* know something was wrong with Drew at the beginning of the halftime show, but by then I couldn't do anything about it.

We'd never done the dip for our salute at a game before, but we'd done it plenty of times in the past week in front of the band. Since we'd stopped falling down, we'd been pretty consistent. He put his hand *there* and his leg *there* and leaned me back until my head almost touched the grass.

The trick was to hold the position for a few seconds, face to face, without cracking each other up. With his hands on me, his dark eyes close to mine, and my heart pounding, it was hard for me not to break into an embarrassed giggle fit. But I managed.

This time was different. He put his hand *there* and his leg *there,* leaned me back, and held me there while the crowd screamed. Our lips almost brushed.

He blinked twice, and I felt myself

falling. He'd lost his balance. He was about to faint. We were going to fall together on the fifty-yard line in front of the entire population of Llama Town.

Then he pulled me up and set me on my feet like nothing had happened.

It took me until halfway through the opening song to recover from the scare. But after that, the show went great. The band sounded awesome. The drums didn't trip themselves up. Drew and I watched each other carefully.

At the end of the show we got a standing ovation. We were the most exciting thing these people had seen since the tractor pull at the county fair.

Our last job was to turn the band to the right and march them off the field. Because some of them wouldn't be able to hear the command over the crowd noise, we'd told them before the show that they would turn to the right.

During the show we took turns. One of us directed the band from the podium while the other directed down on the field. I was on the field now, and Drew was on the podium. He shouted, "Band! Left face!"

Half the band turned to the left because Drew told them to. Half the band turned to the right because they knew they were supposed to.

If he called, "Band, about face," the ones facing left would turn right, but the ones facing right would turn left. I hesitated a split second as I processed this, knowing Drew was thinking the same thing.

Drew swayed a little on the podium.

As casually as possible in knee-high boots and a miniskirt, I ran from my place on the field into the mass of the band. Walking slowly between the lines, I touched each person on the sleeve, saying, "You stay put. You turn around. You stay put. You turn around."

This would take forever. Finally I got wise and called, "Toward the llamas! Everyone turn toward the llamas!"

It worked. The drum cadence started, and the few people who hadn't figured it out yet turned around and followed everyone else out of the stadium. I emerged from the crowd and brought up the rear with Drew.

I didn't say anything to him while we were in the stadium, because we were supposed to be at attention. But as soon as we passed through the fence around the field, I turned to him, angry all over again for the times he'd made me feel like a second-class drum major. "I'm not saying I'll never make a mistake. But I know my left from my right. You're going to get us both fired."

I had some more choice words for him, but by then, Mr. Rush had pushed through the crowd to us. "Morrow," he began. I can't repeat everything he said next. I actually didn't hear all of it over the noise of the Llama Town band playing on the field. But it went something like, "Cussword cussword cussword marching band cussword cussword cussword Pizza Hut cussword cussword cussword Clayton Porridge cuss cuss cuss!"

He blustered away soon enough, and I was about to take another turn at Drew. But his dazed look stopped me. I asked him, "Are you okay?"

"I think I'm coming down with something."

I pulled off my uniform glove, then reached up and pressed my bare hand to his forehead. This was weird. Other than the dip, I'd never touched him on purpose before.

And then I fought the instinct to jerk my hand away in alarm. He was hotter than a human should be.

Temperature. He was hot in temperature. Hot had nothing to do with his dark eyes clouded by fever, or the black curls plastered to his neck with sweat like he'd just enjoyed a long make-out session.

With some lucky flute.

Ugh!

I pulled off the other glove and pressed both my hands on his cheeks to make sure.

He watched me warily like he thought I was about to slap him.

I took my hands away. "Is your throat killing you? It came on all of a sudden? But your head isn't plugged up like a cold?"

He nodded.

"It's probably strep throat. It's been going around. You might even have caught it from me."

"You—" His voice came out a whisper. He cleared his throat and started again. "You haven't been sick."

"I felt it coming on last Sunday. My dad took me to his office and gave me a strep test and antibiotics. You definitely need to go to your doctor tomorrow. If you don't, it could develop into scarlet fever."

"Before eight a.m.?"

"Um, no. But it will just get worse. You won't be in any condition to do anything at eight a.m. Why? Do you have a hot date? Or two?"

He shook his head. "I'm driving to Auburn."

The Auburn University football team had an away game. I asked, "What for?"

"I'm taking the SAT." He swallowed. "Oh, my God, I'm taking the SAT with scarlet fever."

I grasped his gloved hand and led him toward the band's place in the stands. On the way we passed Allison. She glanced down at our hands, then looked at me with both expertly shaped eyebrows raised. I shook my head and asked her to get Drew a Coke.

I sat him down in the stands, then found Mr. Rush with Ms. Martineaux again. "Drew's sick," I said. "Do we bring a first aid kit with us to games? Do you think it might have Tylenol in it?"

"Are you shitting me?"

Ms. Martineaux stared in shock at Mr. Rush, like any sensible person would when he opened his mouth.

He went on, "I'd get sued up, down, and sideways if I gave a child a pill without the school nurse filling out a form in quadruplicate." He turned back to sweet-talk Ms. Martineaux, who now looked like she was not at all sure about this.

I gazed up into the stands next to the band, but I didn't recognize any parents. Nobody but the cheerleaders and the band was stupid enough to come all this way to watch our football team get their butts kicked.

I turned to the clarinets. They were a resourceful lot. "Do y'all have any pain pills on you?"

All the clarinets rummaged through large purses. This amazed me because we weren't allowed to bring purses or bags of any kind into the stadium. If Drew or I had seen them with a purse, we would have sent them back to the bus to get rid of it. A really resourceful lot. They passed a band hat down the line with pills in it.

Allison came back with Drew's Coke and peered into the hat with me. I took some painkillers and the Coke down to Drew.

The Evil Twin already sat beside him.

If she'd brought him a Coke and some Tylenol, I would feel like a fool. A fool in a miniskirt.

But no, she only took up where she left off venting at him because he'd ridden on the freshman bus. With me.

I sat on his other side and handed him the Coke and the pills. While he drank, I leaned across him and said to the twin, "Not right now. He's sick."

Drew choked on the Coke.

I pounded him on the back.

The twin was still going.

When Drew could talk again, he interrupted her in a rough voice, "Really, could you give it a rest? I can't even, like . . ." He squeezed his eyes shut.

"Think?" I suggested.

"I can't even think right now. I'll call you tomorrow."

She left in a huff. Drew and I both took a deep breath and sighed together.

"Why do you let her talk to you like that?" I asked. "It doesn't seem like you."

"You're not supposed to yell at girls," he told me again, hoarsely. "Besides, I've known her forever. I've had class with her since kindergarten. I'm used to it. It rolls off."

"That doesn't explain why you would go out of your way to date it. What are you doing? Trying each flute until you find one who puts out?"

He was quiet so long that I thought I'd pushed him too far and insulted him on a sensitive topic. Maybe he was "sexually active," as they referred to it in the ob-gyn office, with the twin. Yikes!

But then he said, "What are you doing? Using Walter as a human shield so *you* don't have to put out?"

We gave each other a long look. It was like we were back in the farm truck, just the two of us, with the windows rolled up and the band muffled around us. He was dead-on about something I'd only half-realized about myself.

He cleared his throat like it hurt. "I'm dating her because she's pretty and she's nice."

This had not been my experience with

the twins. I didn't challenge the pretty part, but I asked him, "Nice? Which one are you dating?"

"The nice one."

"Which one is that?"

He didn't answer.

"Drew. Do you know which twin you're dating?"

Slowly, like he was sore, he set down his Coke, pulled off his gloves, and ran both hands back through his wet curls. "I've only dated her since the beginning of summer band camp. Five weeks."

"Five weeks is a long time to date someone without knowing her name."

"Right," he said emotionlessly. "It went too far. I can't admit it to her now."

"Why weren't you honest with her in the first place?"

"I should have been. I realized later. I was kind of distracted that week."

I tried to imagine what could distract a boy from figuring out which girl he'd asked to watch TV at the Rent 2 Own. "Distracted by what?"

"You. Drum major stuff. And I had some stuff going on at home."

"Drum major!" the band yelled above

us. Our team had scored a field goal. I jumped up.

Drew was still sitting down. "I'm afraid to stand up," he said.

I directed the fight song for the skeleton crew of drums and trumpets who'd stayed in the stands during third quarter. I kept my eyes on Drew. He must be half dead to sit out the fight song and risk Mr. Rush calling him the *I*-word. But Mr. Rush was absorbed in arguing with Ms. Martineaux.

When I sat down again, Drew leaned his damp head on my shoulder.

I took a long breath, slow enough that he wouldn't notice, I hoped. I told myself that his head on my shoulder didn't mean anything. He was just sick.

I glanced down at his bare hands, and felt a little sick myself. He wasn't wearing a class ring. Almost all senior boys wore one. Unless they had given it away. "Does she have your class ring?" I asked.

"Who?"

"Good question."

"Oh." He held up his hand and examined it. "I don't have a class ring. I ordered one, but we canceled a lot of orders all of a sudden during the summer. Anyway, she and I aren't that serious."

I laughed. "Does *she* know that?"

Luther, Barry, and a few more trombones banged down the stadium stairs and crowded around us. I still thought Luther was cute, and I didn't understand why Allison didn't think so too. Somehow he managed to wear his band uniform in that ultra-casual way he wore all his clothes, even though it was the same uniform everyone else wore.

He poked at Drew with the end of his trombone slide. I think this was a boy version of concern. "What's the matter with you?" he asked.

"I have scarlet fever," Drew said.

"Ooooooh, aaaaaah," the trombones chorused as they ran away.

Only Luther stayed. "You can't be sick. You're taking the SAT tomorrow."

"Helpful, Luther," I said.

Luther studied Drew's head on my shoulder. "Looks like he doesn't need any more help. Drew, you know the Evil Twin won't like this."

Drew shot Luther the bird. I think this was how boys showed appreciation for concern.

Luther cussed at Drew and stomped up the stairs.

Drew nuzzled my shoulder.

By the end of the game his face felt cooler, but he had chills. I tried not to be disappointed. I'd been half-hoping he'd be hot and the shirt would come off again. Instead, he stumbled into the seat at the back of the bus and asked me to borrow a blanket for him.

I used the blanket as a cover to take his band shoes from Allison at the bus door and slip them back into his bag at our feet. But then, over the bus engine starting, I told him, "I don't think the blanket is a good idea. You only *think* you're cold. You don't want to get overheated when you have a fever."

I glanced over at Ariel and Juliet. They watched us like we were the latest Orlando Bloom movie, but maybe they wouldn't tell on us. Surely nobody felt any loyalty to the twin.

And then the lights in the ceiling of the bus blinked out.

"I'll keep you warm," I whispered into the darkness. I wrapped my arm around him.

This seemed fine with Drew. He relaxed into me. I decided I kind of liked this fever thing.

Then he bent down to his bag. He stayed bent for a few long seconds. He must have realized his band shoes were back. Then he shrugged and brought out the SAT book and a little flashlight.

"Not again," I said. "Why are you taking the SAT tomorrow, anyway? You knew you wouldn't get home tonight until one thirty."

"It's the last time I can take it before the scholarship deadline at Auburn."

"Why'd you wait so long to take it, then?"

He sighed the longest sigh. "I took it last fall. I didn't do well on the critical reading. But I did well enough to get into Auburn. I didn't know then that I needed a scholarship." He leaned against me again, heavily, like giving up.

"Do you want me to quiz you?"

He handed me the book and held the flashlight for me. I kept one arm around him and thumbed through the book with the other hand. I found a good word right off. "Captious."

"Finding fault with every little thing."

I thumbed some more. "Vituperate."

"To find fault."

I skipped a whole section of pages to find one he hadn't studied. "Excoriate."

"To denounce severely."

"You know all of these," I said. "Invective."

"An insult."

"Bravado," I said.

"A pretentious display of courage. Do you mean me?"

"Abjure," I said. "Abjure" was like "abdicate." Give up the throne. Give up the drum major position.

Drew didn't recite the definition, but he knew what I was getting at. "You wish," he said. "I can't believe I'm dying of scarlet fever and you're using SAT words to argue with me."

"I'm not using SAT words to argue with you."

"You've got that whole book, and you just happen to vituperate and excoriate and throw invectives at me? And you say my *girlfriend* is evil?"

I had thought it was funny, but now I felt bad. Captious, even.

I leaned down into the aisle and arranged a couple of coolers so that he'd have a footrest. "Switch with me," I said. I slid around him to sit next to the window. "Lie down," I told him.

"Can't. Have to study."

"You won't get a good score if you're sleep deprived, no matter how many words you know. Lie down."

"You have to ask me words," he said. But he lay down with his shoulder on the seat and his head on my thigh. His legs stretched across the coolers in the aisle, and his feet almost touched Ariel in the next seat. The school bus was definitely too small for Drew.

It had to be the most uncomfortable sleeping position ever. Each time the bus braked, he nearly rolled off the seat. Finally he braced himself by putting his hand on my knee.

"Ask me words," he murmured.

I stayed with lullaby words like "genial" and "bonhomie." His answers got softer, and there was a longer and longer silence before he prompted me to ask another. He was asleep.

The whole bus was asleep except me.

There was no way I could fall asleep in the next three hours. My knee under his hand and my thigh under his head were on fire. Gently I ran my fingers through his wiry black curls. In the faint moonglow through the window, I saw him smile a little, eyes still closed, lashes dark against his cheeks.

I liked touching him on purpose.

Ten

When the buses parked at the high school, Drew was burning up again. It had been about four hours since he took a pill. I dug more of the clarinet stash from my pocket and gave him a drink out of my cooler.

Clearly he was in no shape to drive himself home. I would ask Luther to give him a ride. But by the time we climbed down the stairs of the empty bus, almost all the cars had left the parking lot.

And then I had a better idea. Dad was on call, which meant that he might be at the hospital delivering a baby. If he was home, though, he could start Drew on antibiotics. Drew would still be sick tomorrow at 8 a.m., but at least he might be on the road to recovery, with the edge taken off the fever. Not stupid-sick like he was now, and getting worse.

Allison was asleep in the passenger side of my car. Without arguing with me, Drew stretched out on the backseat, and I drove to my house.

When I parked in the driveway, Allison got out of the car and wandered over to her house without saying good-bye or taking her stuff. Her bags and boots and sequined leotard and tiara sat in the passenger seat like a pool of melted majorette. Drew didn't wake up.

Inside the house Dad dozed on the couch with the Weather Channel on. I pinched him a little harder than necessary, and he started up. I explained the situation with Drew.

"I can't just give him an antibiotic," Dad said. "He has to take a strep test first."

"Do you have one on you? Come on, Dad. They're my germs. It's my fault if he gets a three-twenty on the critical reading."

I followed Dad as he grabbed a flashlight from a drawer and walked out to the car. When he opened the back door, Drew still didn't wake up.

"Drew," Dad said gently.

Drew opened his eyes and sat up. "Hello, Dr. Sauter."

I wondered how Drew knew Dad. Of course, most people did. Dad and Allison's dad were well known. They'd delivered half the town.

"Open your mouth and say 'ah,'" Dad told him. He used the flashlight to peer into Drew's throat. "Good news," he said, clicking the flashlight off. "You're not pregnant."

I was horrified at Dad for the stupid joke. It was bad enough that he was an ob-gyn. He didn't have to go around reminding people.

But Drew laughed. And laughed. And laughed. He was really sick.

Dad rolled his eyes and closed the car door. "Does he live across town? You can't take him home. Let him borrow your car. Your mother will take you to get it tomorrow."

"I don't think he should drive, Dad. He's comatose."

"Well, *you're* not driving him. It would be past two before you got home."

"Can you drive him?"

"Hell, no. I'm on call." Being on call made him testy. "He can stay in the guest room."

"What about the antibiotic?"

"Maybe. I'll call his mother."

How embarrassing. "You don't even *know* his mother."

"She's my patient. I just saw her yesterday." He went into the house.

I opened the car door again. Drew had fallen asleep sitting up.

"Drew," I said.

Slowly he opened his eyes and turned to me. His expression changed. I recognized that dark-eyed look. It was the same look he'd given me last Tuesday at practice, when I accused him of being innocent.

I understood what the look meant now. Drew wasn't innocent. He was anything but.

Ever so briefly, I thought about what it would be like to make out with a feverish Drew in the backseat of my car.

I might have tried to find out, too, if Dad hadn't been just inside the house, *on the phone with Drew's mother.*

"Come on." I took Drew's hand and pulled.

He didn't budge. Instead, *he* pulled *me,* and kept me standing beside the car.

I thought he might pull me *into* the car. He couldn't quite decide.

He swallowed, and winced.

"You're sick," I whispered.

He slid off the seat and let me lead him across the driveway, into the house, and onto the living room couch. When we sat down next to each other, I released my grip on his hand.

But he didn't release his grip on mine.

And then he moved his thumb up to the tip of my thumb and down the other side.

A chill washed over me.

He reversed direction and moved his thumb to the tip of my thumb again, down into the sensitive hollow between my thumb and finger. Up to my fingertip and down the other side. Up to the next fingertip and down the other side. Over and over, all the way to my pinky, where he reversed direction and did it again.

I stared at my hand open to his hand. I glanced up at him once, but he was watching our hands too. So it wasn't some kind of feverish spasm. He knew what he was doing.

I could hear Dad still talking on the phone in the kitchen. I willed Dad to stay on the phone for a really long time. I stopped breathing every time Drew's thumb neared my fingertip. And each time his thumb dipped into the hollow between my fingers, a new chill washed from my face, down my neck, down my arms, and all the way to my toes.

A *beep* sounded as Dad hung up the phone. I jerked my hand back into my lap.

Dad walked into the living room. "It's a go," he said. "Drew, you look better."

And just like that, it was over. Dad found Drew an antibiotic, and I gave him a glass of water. Then I prodded him toward the guest bedroom. He stretched out on the bed without looking back at me, and without pulling down the covers. He was already gone. There didn't seem to be much point in suggesting that he take off his Vans. I found another blanket in the closet, covered him, turned off the light, and left the room, closing the door behind me.

And stood there staring at the closed door. I was like an amputee who still thought her missing leg was there. I could feel his cheek on my thigh and his hand on my knee and his thumb tracing up and down the outline of my hand.

I should have hated him for his snarky comment when we first got on the bus: *If it weren't for you, there wouldn't be a problem.* I should have hated him for making me feel like Mini-Me. I knew he just had a fever, he was out of his mind, he wanted some lovin', and I was convenient. If he really liked me and wanted to date me, he would have broken up with the twin by now.

I knew all this. And he *still* had me lit up like the Fourth of July. In September.

I went to my room and changed into pajamas. Then changed into different pajamas. Actually stood in front of the full-length mirror to see what I looked like in pajamas. I was going crazy.

Then there was the bra. I couldn't wear a bra to bed. I'd suffocate in my sleep. But what if Drew got up and needed something during the night? I couldn't let him see me without a bra. Finally I put on my bra and left it unfastened.

I curled up on the couch in the living room, with the guest room door just down the hall. Drew's cheek still burned a hole through my thigh, his hand through my knee. His thumb crested my fingertips and sank into the hollows between my fingers. The Weather Channel and the threat of a turbulent front on the way lulled me to sleep.

Eleven

The shower in the hall bathroom woke me. My mouth was wide open. Drew had walked across the hall from the guest room to the bathroom. He'd probably looked in here and seen me snoring.

I jumped to the mirror above the fireplace to make sure there wasn't any drool on my face, at least. Then I passed my hands across my cheeks and fingered my hair down where it stuck up in back.

I never wore makeup, and my hair was short and easy to fix. There was no reason for me to worry about Drew seeing me when I first woke up. I didn't look much different from how I looked at school. I worried anyway. I even thought about running to my room and changing into a tight T-shirt and jeans. But that might make it seem like I cared.

Mom flowed downstairs in full makeup, with her hair already coiffed. My friends bought their mothers flowered robes and fuzzy high-heeled slippers for their birthdays as a joke, to wear when they broke out the toning masks and had spa day. My mother bought this stuff for herself and wore it every day, no joke. Every day was spa day at Chez Sauter.

I followed her into the kitchen, set the table, and helped her start breakfast. Soon Dad sat down in his business clothes and a tie, ready to go to the hospital to make rounds.

Then Drew, looking pale under his tan. He pushed the SAT book across the table to me. He must have gone out this morning and fished it from the car. Or maybe he'd retrieved it during the night and slept with it stuck to his forehead on the off chance some of it would seep into his brain.

"Ignominy," I said, crunching bacon.

"I don't know that one," Mom said.

"Dishonor," Drew said.

I flipped through the pages. "Nefarious," I said.

"I don't know that one," Mom said.

"Wicked," Drew said.

"Atrocity," I said.

"I don't know that one," Mom said. For being crowned Miss State of Alabama 1982, Mom won a full college scholarship. She dropped out of college to get her Mrs. degree and work to put Dad through medical school. Since then, reading *Vogue* was the only exercise she gave her poor cerebrum. Possibly she only looked at the pictures.

"A savagely cruel act," Drew said. "Or something in shockingly bad taste."

I glanced up at him. He was eating, and answering these definitions without thinking. I examined the book closely to find a word that was both difficult and appropriate. "Opprobrious," I said.

"Disgraceful or shameful," said Drew. "I thought we'd called a truce. You're fighting with me with SAT words again."

"She's not doing it for your benefit," Dad butted in. "She's doing it for mine." He reached across the table, jerked the SAT book from my hands, and thumbed through it. "Aha. Vendetta."

"A long and bitter feud," Drew said.

"You know this stuff cold." Dad handed the book back to me without looking at me.

This time I had a word in mind. I'd thought about Dad when I came across it in English class. I looked it up, then read, "Mountebank."

"A quack who isn't what he seems to be," Drew said.

Dad got up and took his half-full plate to the sink.

Mom protested, "You're not going to eat?"

"Not hungry," Dad grumbled, walking back upstairs.

My mom gave me a disapproving look, but she didn't say anything. She'd always stayed out of the fight between me and Dad, even though it had everything to do with her.

Drew stared after Dad, then wisely changed the subject. Waving at a shelf full of trophies and sashes and pictures of me wearing makeup, he asked, "Am I hallucinating?"

"No," I said. "I was Miss Junior East-Central Alabama 2004. I tried to throw all this stuff out, but Mom commandeered it and displayed it in her kitchen to spite me."

Mom said, "You don't want to throw out all those good memories just because you're going through a phase."

"See?" I said. "My mother is the one hallucinating."

Mom huffed out a dainty sigh and stood, putting her manicured hand on Drew's arm. "I'll make you some coffee."

"What!" I exclaimed. "You don't let me drink coffee."

"Drew is older than you," she called from the kitchen.

"He's *seventeen*!"

Drew smirked at me.

"It'll stunt your growth," I told him.

"I'm six foot two. So, you don't get along with your dad?"

"Perspicacious," I said.

"Having keen insight."

I glared at him.

"Oh," he said. "You mean me."

"I liked you a lot better when you had a fever."

The doorbell rang, probably Drew's father. Dad came downstairs again to answer the door. Mom floated in and handed Drew a travel mug. He thanked her so much for her hospitality, blah blah blah.

As he walked toward the door, Mom held me back. "He has very good manners. He seems like a nice boy," she whispered, like I'd intended to bring him home to meet the parents.

Of course he seemed like a nice boy. Mom would think Eminem seemed like a nice boy compared to Walter. Walter had perfectly good manners too, but Walter lived in a bus. It was hard for people to get past the bus.

Out on the front porch Dad and Drew talked with Drew's father. He must have come straight from the night shift at the mill. He was covered in a thin white film, and larger clumps of cotton stuck to the back of his hair and his work shirt.

Drew motioned to his dad's car, and I followed him. He bent his head down close to me and said quietly, "Thank you."

"For what? Strep throat?"

He frowned. "Why won't you let me thank you? What's happened? Are you acting this way because I asked you about your dad?"

There was no way he'd forgotten about

what he was doing with his hand the night before. If I'd felt what I felt, he had to have felt *something,* no matter how out of it he was.

I folded my arms on my chest. "Good luck."

He looked at me like he wanted something else from me. But I didn't have anything more to give him just then. Except the SAT book.

Dad and I watched the car climb the brick driveway. Little cotton fibers hung in the bright, still air and glinted in the sun.

"He seems like a nice boy," Dad said.

"He is *not* a nice boy. He just acted that way this morning because he's delirious."

"You might give him a break. He's going through a hard time with his family right now."

A hard time? Letting down the Morrow family drum major legacy? "What kind of hard time?" I asked. Then I remembered what Drew had told me on the bus about why he hadn't bothered to figure out which twin he was dating. He was distracted by stuff going on at home.

Dad shook his head. "If he hasn't told you, I can't tell you."

Drew's mother was Dad's patient. Dad couldn't give away his patients' secrets. I considered all the things that could be wrong with Drew's mother that would give Drew a hard time at home. Ovarian cancer. Breast cancer. I asked, "Is she going to die?"

Dad blinked. "No. Just give him a break, would you? Forgive and forget?"

Dad was asking me to give Drew a break. But I knew what he meant. Dad wanted a break for himself.

Twelve

Drew was out of school Monday and Tuesday. The Evil Twins were out too. I was very thankful I didn't have to deal with them without Drew there to run interference for me. And I was glad they'd missed their hot date at the Rent 2 Own.

But I was jealous of their germs. I wondered what Drew had done with the twins to give them strep, and when. Then I remembered that it had been going around school for weeks. And when Luther came down with it on Wednesday, I felt much better.

Except that Drew was still acting like the whole hand thing hadn't happened. He was nice to me like he was supposed to be.

He even flirted with me a little during practice, and seemed hurt when I didn't flirt back.

I lived for him to flirt with me, and I wanted so badly to flirt back. I lived for him to touch me *there* and *there* when we practiced the dip.

But I felt used. He still hadn't broken up with the twins. What did he think I was, some trashy hand-slut? I felt like he'd taken advantage of me for a good time and then dumped me. But he *hadn't* taken advantage of me. He'd hardly done *anything.* And I couldn't decide whether that made it better or worse. Which made me even madder.

Everyone was back at school on Friday, in time for homecoming. Sure enough, Allison was a candidate for Miss Homecoming/Miss Victory. So was Tracey Reardon.

I couldn't believe it. People hated the twins. Or maybe they just hated Cacey. But as I asked around, I found out that one or both of them had run a one-woman or two-woman public relations campaign of their own. They got some credit because they dated Drew, who was high profile. Plus, lots of boys apparently thought the mean Avril-Lavigne-on-steroids attitude was a turn-on.

The announcement came at the end of my English class, just before lunch on Friday. Allison got the most votes. She was Miss Homecoming. Tracey was next. She was Miss Victory.

At the bell I rushed out of the room and down to the lunchroom, where I always met Allison. She waved and grinned at me from way down the hall. Then, as I watched, one of the twins stopped her, said something to her, and flounced away.

Allison didn't react. She started walking again as if nothing had happened. And then, when I reached her, I saw that her eyes were hard.

"What did she say to you?" I breathed.

Allison shook her head. "I hate this town, I hate this town, I hate this town."

"Oh, God, Allison. *What did she say to you?*"

Allison licked her perfect lipstick. She said woodenly, "'Tracey Reardon isn't going to be Miss Victory. A white girl doesn't have to take a black girl's leavings.'"

I went cold in the crowded, muggy hallway. All I could think of to say was, "Ick!" Then, "She's Miss Icktory."

Allison didn't laugh. She still looked stunned.

I pushed her into the lunchroom and through the line. I even loaded her salad plate for her, avoiding the beets. At one of the tables Drew laughed with Luther, Barry, and the other trombones. I shoved Allison along in front of me and sat her down there.

This was partly chance. There happened to be a couple of empty seats at the end of their table, probably because everyone was afraid of the trombones poking fun at them. But I also wanted Drew to know what his twins had done. I told the whole table what had happened.

"She said that?" Drew asked incredulously.

Luther reached across the table and whacked Drew on the arm. "You're dating a racist."

"You don't know that." Drew turned to Allison. "Which one of the twins said it?"

She shrugged.

"Why does it matter which one said

it?" I asked him. "What will that tell you? You don't even know which one you're dating."

"I *do* know which one I'm dating," he said triumphantly. "I figured that out this morning in homeroom. I know I'm dating the one who isn't on the homecoming court. I'm dating Cacey."

The trombones clapped for him.

He turned to Allison again. "What exactly did she say?"

I had been worried about Allison, but now I felt better. She came back to life and got angry. Her voice louder with every word, she repeated, "'Tracey Reardon. Isn't going to be. Miss Victory. A white girl. Doesn't have to take. A black girl's. *Leavings!*'"

"Abjure," I said under my breath to Drew.

He didn't look at me, but I knew from the way his jaw tightened that he'd heard me.

"If she said 'Tracey Reardon,' then she must have been Cacey," Luther pointed out. "Drew, you have to break up with—" His voice trailed off.

My heart beat faster at the thought that

Drew was going to break up with her. He was finally going to break up with her! He was as good as mine!

Then I saw that Drew had borrowed Mr. Rush's brain-melting stare and was giving it to Luther.

"It wasn't necessarily Cacey," Barry joined in helpfully. "It might have been Tracey. She could have referred to herself in the third person like small children do. Like Elmo on *Sesame Street*."

"Right. Let's think about this scientifically," said Luther. He instructed Barry to get out his notebook and draw a grid. Then he asked Allison, "What was she wearing?"

Allison closed her eyes. "Jeans and one of those new school spirit T-shirts."

"They both are," Drew muttered. The furious look in his eyes had faded. But he was avoiding everyone's gaze, examining the water-stained ceiling.

"How about something else that distinguishes them from each other?" Luther prompted Allison. "Earrings, or shoes?"

"I didn't notice," Allison said, putting her hand to her forehead. "I was kind of preoccupied with this girl questioning my right to breathe her air."

Luther moved closer to her. "This is important. We may be able to track her if we can figure out that, say, Tracey carries a pink bag and Cacey carries a red one."

"They both wear bad blue eyeliner," I offered, "but I think it's Cacey who sometimes experiments with green." I was making this up.

"That's good," Luther said, pointing at me. "Barry, write that down. Allison, did her eyeliner jump out at you?"

I asked, "How could it not?"

"Now you're being captious," Drew said to me.

"Don't you dare excoriate me," I said. "You're the one with the nefarious girlfriend."

Craig Coley and some of the other trombones at the end of the table talked low together, looking up often at Drew.

Drew's eyes focused on me like he wanted to say something else to me. Then his glance slid off me to Craig. "What, Craig? Bring it on."

"You're the leader of the band, Drew," Craig said. "Not just the half of the band that's white."

"Don't tell me what to do," Drew said.

"Drew, you have to break up with her," said Luther. "Serious."

"Back off," Drew told Luther. He turned to me. "You're loving this, aren't you?"

"No. I'm not loving what she did to Allison. Where *is* your girlfriend, anyway? Why don't you go find her? Why don't you go comfort her in this time of great sorrow for her and/or her sister?"

"Good idea." He got up, towering over the table, and walked across the lunchroom. He stopped at the table where both twins in their matching school spirit T-shirts sat with some of their friends.

Aww, man! I hadn't expected him to take my suggestion. But I should have known he'd want to discuss the situation with the twins like responsible adults.

I turned to Allison to see if she was feeling better. But she was watching Drew. So was Luther. The whole table watched Drew as he bent to talk to the twins with his arms crossed on his chest.

"When he comes back," Luther said quietly, "I'd advise you ladies to cool it a little. We know Drew isn't a racist. He'll do the right thing. He just doesn't want to break up with her on hearsay. But he's under a lot of pressure right now. If you push him too hard, he's liable to snap." He snapped his fingers.

I insisted, "I am not going to tiptoe around Drew Morrow just because he wants to hang on to long hair, big boobs, and her sister."

Drew walked back toward us, arms crossed, and didn't uncross them until he pulled out his chair and sat down. He hardly glanced at me as he announced to the table in general, "She said she would never make a comment like that."

"Which one?" I asked.

Barry and Craig and the other trombones snorted with laughter. Luther gave them a warning look.

Drew glared at me. "Both of them."

"Well, one of them is lying," I said. "Or Allison is lying. Who do you believe?"

He looked over at the twins' table, where the twins and all their friends were watching *our* table. Then he turned to Allison, as if he were really pondering the question: Allison versus Evil Twins. "Everyone is attacking me when I didn't do anything," he said, again to the table instead of me. "It's not fair."

"How do you think Allison feels?" I asked.

Allison raised her carefully shaped eyebrows at him.

He reached across the table, covered her hand with his hand, and squeezed. "I know," he said. "But you're acting like *I* did something awful, when I didn't."

"Ouch ouch ouch ouch!" she squealed, pulling her hand from under his and shaking it out. She examined her manicure.

"Sorry." He finally turned back to me. "I'm sorry, but I wouldn't do something like that, and neither would Tracey."

"You're dating Cacey!" called the table.

His jaw was set. "I said back off."

Luther sat up straight and clapped his hands. "Drew says back off. I trust him to investigate and to do the right thing."

"You didn't trust him a few minutes ago when you had Barry charting the twins' wardrobes," I said. "You're going to let Drew get away with this just because you're afraid he's going to blow?"

"Back. Off," Drew told me.

"Me! Why don't you tell the twin to

back off Allison? What do you see in that racist, anyway? Why don't you break up with her?"

"Virginia," Allison said in warning.

Drew shouted at me, "Don't tell me what to do!"

"Drew," said Luther, looking over our shoulders.

It occurred to me that Luther and Allison might see a twin behind us. But I didn't care anymore. I screamed at Drew, "You're not supposed to yell at girls!"

I felt someone close at my shoulder. I whirled around to tell Tracey/Cacey exactly what I thought of her/them.

It was Mr. Rush.

I braced for him to let us have it. But he glanced over to Ms. Martineaux at the teacher table. Then he said quietly, "I thought we agreed you kids would play nice."

Drew shouted at Mr. Rush, "Take a number!"

I slapped my hand over Drew's mouth.

The lunchroom had fallen so silent that I could hear air hissing in the ceiling duct-work and pots clanking way back in the kitchen. Drew's chest rose and fell quickly under my arm, and I could feel his heart thumping.

Mr. Rush spoke slowly through his teeth. "I am *busy with my colleagues*. Go wait for me outside my office. I'll be down there when I wrap this up. And while you're walking, enjoy your last five minutes as drum majors."

Thirteen

Drew and I tried to escape the hushed lunchroom as quickly as possible. But of course the lunchroom lady stood guard at the door. We had to go all the way back to our table, take our trays all the way to the dishwasher, and walk all the way back through the lunchroom with the entire band and a hundred other people watching our every move. Clayton Porridge seemed especially interested.

We walked down to the band room without talking. Drew naturally walked faster than me, and I let him get ahead.

When I pushed open the heavy door to the band room, Drew was pacing. I put my back against Mr. Rush's office door, slid to the floor, kicked off my flip-flops, and took my drumsticks out of my backpack.

Drew paced from the instrument storage room to Mr. Rush's office and back. It was annoying, but I was sure I could be more annoying if I tried. The more he paced, the louder I tapped with my drumsticks on the floor.

Finally he paused in front of me. "Can you stop that?"

"Don't tell me what to do," I mimicked him over the tapping. "I'm hungry. Aren't you? We should never argue at lunch."

He bent down toward me with his hand extended. "May I borrow those?"

I handed over the drumsticks in surprise. If I'd had time to think about it, I wouldn't have given them to him, because I could have predicted what he'd do.

Sure enough, he reared back with his arm and threw the drumsticks hard. They sailed across the band room, clattered against the far wall, and rang some cymbals on their way down to the carpet.

When Drew wheeled back around, Mr.

Rush stood in the band room doorway with his arms folded.

"Fire me, then!" Drew shouted at Mr. Rush. "Just go ahead and fire me!"

"I don't want to fire you, Morrow," Mr. Rush said. "Or Sauter, either. Have you *seen* Clayton Porridge?" He unlocked the door-knob over my head.

He sat down at his desk, and I sat down in a chair. He told Drew, "Better close the door, despite the repercussions."

Drew pulled the door closed, then stood behind the empty chair.

"Please have a seat," Mr. Rush said.

"No thanks," Drew said.

"Sit!"

Drew sat down.

"Now then," Mr. Rush began pleas-antly—so pleasantly that I knew he was faking. "Why don't you tell me what the problem is?"

I piped up, "He's dating a racist—"

"You don't *know* that," Drew said.

"—and he's just too stubborn to admit it."

Mr. Rush put his chin in his hand and considered me. "What business is it of yours who he's dating?"

Drew didn't say "Yeah!" but he didn't

have to. I could feel him staring at me smugly.

"His girlfriend made a racist comment to my friend," I said.

Mr. Rush moved his hand away from his chin so he could gape at me. "Oh, shit. We are *not* going to have any of *that* going on in my marching band. Which twin was it?"

"We don't know!" Drew shouted in exasperation.

Mr. Rush turned to Drew. "You mean you can't tell them apart?" He chuckled. "Sounds like true love, Morrow. But this isn't why you two are fighting. It's the subject matter of the hour, but it's not *why*." He rubbed his hands together. "I think I know of something that can help us. Now, it may surprise you to hear that I come from a dysfunctional family."

"No!" Drew said sarcastically.

"Watch it, Morrow. Anyway, one of the times the police came, the judge sent us to family counseling. Despite the fact that I was a jaded teen at the time, I found family counseling very enlightening."

He leaned forward in his chair. "It's simple. You don't interrupt each other.

You let the person talking say their peace. You take turns telling each other how you feel."

"Drew and I tried this last Friday on the bus," I said. "It didn't work out. We didn't speak to each other again until Drew's temperature went up to a hundred and four."

"She's easier to get along with when she's blurry," Drew said.

Mr. Rush gave Drew the evil eye, then turned it on me. He went on as if we hadn't interrupted him. "Here's how family counseling works. You start, 'I feel,' and put in an emotion, and then tell us why you feel that way. Sauter, you go first."

Immediately I said, "I feel angry."

"Too easy," said Mr. Rush.

"I feel," I said again. Clearly, we were not going to get out of this until Mr. Rush thought we were making some sort of effort. So I considered how I really felt. As I reached deep down, I was surprised by what I found in there.

"Time's up," said Drew. "Game over."

"Shut up!" Mr. Rush and I both yelled at him.

"I feel proud," I said quickly. "Of Drew."

Drew's eyes met mine, but I couldn't say the rest of this while I looked at him. I turned to Mr. Rush.

"I like Drew." Understatement of the year. "Drew is a terrific drum major. Working with a partner has been hard for him after he was drum major by himself last year. All things considered, I think he's handled it pretty well. Except that pesky problem of not knowing his left from his right—"

"I had a fever!"

"Don't interrupt," said Mr. Rush.

"And I feel proud of myself," I went on. "It's been hard on me, too. I never expected to be drum major this year. There have been times when I wanted to give it up. But I could never give it up after Mr. O'Toole acted like a girl couldn't do it. I've proven that a girl can do it. Now any girl can do it. Ariel James can try out if she wants to."

"Yeah, I've got my eye on James for drum major a few years down the road," Mr. Rush said. "She keeps writing concertos and handing them in to me for no apparent

153

reason. Some kind of idiot savant."

"I thought you weren't supposed to interrupt me," I said.

"Seriously," Mr. Rush said to Drew. "Does James talk?"

"No," said Drew.

"Maybe that's because you don't let her get a word in edgewise!" I shouted. Now that I'd started this "I feel" crap, I wasn't letting go. "I feel frustrated!"

"Tell us why you feel frustrated," Mr. Rush said calmly.

"I feel frustrated because Drew and I have different styles of drum majoring. I discuss things with people. Drew yells at people." I realized I was still yelling myself, and lowered my voice. "I think both styles could work. But Drew won't let me find out whether my style works. Every time I try to solve a problem by discussing things with people, Drew comes up behind me and yells. And if one drum major is discussing something with you but the other drum major is yelling at you, you're naturally going to obey the one yelling at you."

Drew started, "I don't—"

"Nnnn," said Mr. Rush, waving a hand at Drew.

"It's like I'm the mother," I said, "and Drew is the father who shouts all the time. I don't want to be the mother."

"Do you want to be the father?" Drew asked.

"I'm too young to be either. I want to be the freaking drum major!"

I tried to slow my breathing down. I felt like an idiot, getting all worked up. And I expected Mr. Rush and Drew to make sarcastic comments about it.

But Mr. Rush just considered me soberly, slowly clicking a ballpoint pen open and closed, like he took this very seriously.

I could feel Drew staring at me too. I was afraid to look in his direction and see that smirk still on his face. Finally I turned to Drew, ready to defend myself. But he looked serious too. Like it mattered to him how I felt.

Mr. Rush leaned back in his chair and put his pen down. "That's great, Sauter. Morrow, do you have a response to this?"

Still eyeing me, Drew said, "I don't come up behind her and yell when she's talking to people."

"Sauter," Mr. Rush said, "can you give Morrow some examples of times when he's done this?"

"Last Friday when I was getting us into the backseat of the bus. Last Friday when I was breaking up a fight on the bus. Wednesday when the trumpets started the lawn mower and rode it around the football field. Yesterday—"

"That's enough," Mr. Rush said.

"You're not supposed to interrupt," I said.

"We don't have all day," Mr. Rush said. "We've got to practice the homecoming parade eventually. Morrow, now that Sauter has listed your offenses, can you see you're doing this?"

"Yes," Drew told me.

"And can you make an effort to quit stepping on her toes?"

Drew closed his eyes. "Yes."

"Great," said Mr. Rush. "One problem solved. What else, Sauter?"

I should have just left it there. But a girl doesn't get this kind of opportunity with a boy very often. The opportunity to make him *explain* himself.

"I feel confused," I said. "About the hand."

Mr. Rush looked from me to Drew and back. "Go on."

"Drew knows what I mean."

Mr. Rush and I both turned to Drew.

Drew shrugged. "I don't even remember the hand."

"Obviously you do," I said, "or you wouldn't know what I'm talking about."

Mr. Rush came halfway out of his chair to lean across the desk in Drew's direction. "You're about to be in big trouble, Morrow. I told you that if you hurt my drum major—"

"I didn't hurt her," Drew said. Jaw set, he was getting angry again. "I wouldn't hurt her."

"Then where did you have your hand?" Mr. Rush asked suspiciously.

"On her *hand*."

Mr. Rush sat down, looking dumbfounded. At a loss for words. For once. Then he snorted. "Morrow, we need to have a talk."

"Luther already told me that," Drew said.

"Who?" Mr. Rush's brow wrinkled in confusion.

"Washington," Drew said.

"Oh yeah," Mr. Rush said. "Trombone section leader, right? I think he's responsible for that blasted 'ooooooh, aaaaaah.' Unless *you* started it."

Drew blinked innocently.

"I want my question answered," I said.

"I don't think you're going to get an honest answer until we work out some of the bigger stuff," Mr. Rush told me. "Why don't you tell us about piercing your nose?"

I was tempted. But there was no way I could tell Mr. Rush about my dad. "Let Drew have a turn."

Mr. Rush and I turned to Drew expectantly.

Drew shook his head like he couldn't believe this was happening. Finally he said, "I feel . . . threatened."

Mr. Rush said, "No shit."

Drew glared at him.

"Sorry," said Mr. Rush. "Totally inappropriate comment from the family counselor. Go on."

Drew ran his hands back through his dark hair. I knew we were about to find out about the stuff going on at home.

"I always thought I was going to

college," he said. "My parents had a college fund for me. Then my mother got pregnant. And in August my parents told me she's pregnant with twins."

What a relief! His mother didn't have cancer. She wasn't dying of anything. But I could see how getting two new siblings when he was seventeen years old would cause huge problems for Drew.

And of course I said the perfect thing to comfort him. "Are you a Gemini?"

"Sauter," Mr. Rush scolded me. Then he said to Drew, "I think I see what the matter is. You were the youngest child. The irresponsible black sheep of the Morrow Mafia. Now, without warning, you're Jan Brady."

"Who?" Drew asked.

"The middle child from *The Brady Bunch*," I said.

"The pretty one?" Drew asked.

"No," Mr. Rush and I said together.

"That's not it," Drew said. "Well, sort of. But the bigger thing is that my mother's having health problems. It's hard on your body to have twins, especially when you're forty-two. She had to quit her job. So we're low on money.

My father's working all the overtime he can get at the mill. And I can't have my college fund."

He swallowed and ran his hands through his hair again. "They're telling me I have to do my work plus Dad's work on the farm. I have to get a high score on the SAT and get a scholarship, or I can't go to college. I have to be responsible. But I wasn't the one who was irresponsible in the first place. How is all of this my responsibility? I wasn't even in the same county. I was at an Auburn baseball game with Luther while my parents were drinking one too many margaritas and having sex without using birth control."

Mr. Rush cleared his throat and stood. "Morrow, I think we've made a lot of progress this session, and you can pay my hundred and fifty dollars to the receptionist—"

"You started this!" Drew yelled.

"You're right," Mr. Rush said, sitting down.

Drew lowered his voice. "I don't know what I got on the SAT. I did the best I could. I need to stay drum major so my extracurricular activities will show a position of responsibility. I've done the best I could as drum major. It was the only sure thing I had left. Last year I got high marks at all three contests, and I won two of them. But for all that, Mr. O'Toole demoted me. He made me co–drum major. And now"— he gestured to Mr. Rush—"you keep threatening to fire me. Was I supposed to win the third contest? Would that have been good enough?"

"Don't take it personally, Morrow," said Mr. Rush. "I was only manipulating you."

Drew didn't react to what Mr. Rush said. He looked straight ahead, through Mr. Rush. "My granddad worked his whole life in the cotton mill. My dad has worked his whole life in the cotton mill. There was no way I was going to work in that cotton mill, ever."

He closed his eyes, took in a long breath, and let it out slowly. His shoulders sagged. He said quietly, "I wanted to go to veterinary school."

"Lots of people go to the junior college for the first two years, to save money," I suggested. "Then they transfer to Auburn."

"Both my brothers went to the junior college," Drew said, nodding. "And do you know what they're doing now?"

I winced. "Working in the cotton mill?"

"They're working in the cotton mill!" He was shaking. I wondered if his father had ever allowed him to get this upset in his life.

Drew said to the filing cabinet behind Mr. Rush, "God, they keep after me all the time, telling me what to do, and telling me how irresponsible I am. Sometimes I start to believe it. I should go ahead and get a job in the mill. It's inevitable anyway, right? Drop out of school. Move in with my brother. Send my parents money to pay them back for raising me. Help finance their new push to populate the earth."

I looked at Mr. Rush in alarm.

He shook his head at me: *Don't worry.*

Don't worry! I put my hand over Drew's trembling hand on the edge of his chair, and squeezed, and didn't let go. Then I asked Mr. Rush, "Did they teach you to do this in your education classes in college?"

"No," Mr. Rush said. "In fact, if my

advisor saw this, she'd shit right now."

"You're not listening to me!" Drew shouted.

"Yes, we are," Mr. Rush said in a soothing psychiatrist voice I'd never heard from him. Like he'd learned something in his education classes after all.

"No, you're not," Drew said. "You're from Big Pine. Big Pine doesn't have a cotton mill."

"Big Pine has a paper mill," Mr. Rush said in the same low voice. "My dad works in the paper mill."

I saw then that Mr. Rush might talk tough to Drew, and Drew might lash back at Mr. Rush, but they got from each other something they didn't get from the men in their families.

They understood each other.

In his normal voice Drew said, "I feel . . . better." He squeezed my hand back and looked over at me, half-smiling.

"Isn't that amazing?" Mr. Rush said. "Talking about your feelings helps you let go of your anger. And it takes a lot of energy to be angry all the time."

"You should know," I said.

"I'm working on it. I need to work on it some more because Martineaux thinks I'm a nutcase."

I jumped as the heavy door to the band room crashed open. The line of boys dropped instrument cases on the floor with periodic *thunks,* and a saxophone player warmed up with scales and arpeggios. Just like the day in Drew's truck, it had seemed for the last half hour like the world had been shut out, and there was no one but me and Drew.

And—oh yeah—our insane band director.

Mr. Rush stood up behind his desk. But I wasn't ready to go. I couldn't bare my feelings to Drew (and our insane band director), and listen to Drew bare his feelings to me (and our insane band director), and suddenly face the band again like snapping my fingers. I didn't think Drew could either.

I let Drew's hand go and slipped my arm protectively around him.

Mr. Rush got my message. "I'll be in big trouble if I let you make out in my office."

"I feel fed up," I told him. "Would you please stop saying that Drew and I are making out or feeling each other up? Would you please stop trying to trick Drew into saying he thinks I'm pretty? Drew and I are friends. Just friends."

Mr. Rush gave me the stare.

And this time I had to look away.

He stood there for a moment more. Just long enough to make me feel as uncomfortable as possible. Then he said, "I'll go direct band practice. Remember the band? The marching band?" He opened the office door, letting in the giggles of freshman girls and the loud honks of the trombone chasing them. "Come out when you're ready." He closed the door behind him.

When Mr. Rush was with us and I'd held Drew's hand, I was just trying to hold Drew steady. Now that Drew and I were alone again, the tingle returned. I rubbed my hand on his back, and fire shot up my arm.

He took several long, slow breaths, like he was trying to collect himself. Then he turned to me. His dark eyes glistened. He said again, "I feel better."

I reached out a finger to touch a tear at the corner of his lashes.

He shook his head and rubbed his eyes. Then he looked around on the floor beneath his chair.

"Did you lose your shoes again?" I asked.

"No, my bravado." He laughed. "I know I left it around here somewhere."

Fourteen

Allison looked beautiful reigning over the homecoming float, and of course she had the pageant smile and the pageant wave down pat. Sure enough, Tracey refused to ride on the float as Miss Victory. Good riddance. The homecoming committee pulled the crepe paper letters spelling MISS VICTORY out of the chicken wire on the back of the float and replaced them with white toilet paper before the parade started.

The parade went great. The band sounded terrific, and the crowd cheered wildly as we passed through the downtown streets, as if we did not suck. Drew and I were relieved because we hadn't practiced the parade formation very much. We'd been too busy perfecting the halftime show for the contest the next weekend.

Then, at the homecoming game, the halftime show went great. This was the first game our hometown crowd had seen us in non-suck-o mode. When Drew and I did the dip, I felt the force of the crowd's noise hit me in the side of the face. And at the end of the show, they went crazy again. The standing ovation was longer and louder than the one in Llama Town.

Drew and I brought up the rear of the band marching off the field. As soon as we passed through the fence, we turned to each other and grabbed each other in a long hug.

Even though we did not like each other as more than friends. Because Drew was dating Miss Icktory's twin sister.

And then, over Drew's shoulder, I saw Walter.

Or did I? He looked like Walter, but older. He'd gotten taller. And he'd grown a beard.

I'd already let Drew go in surprise at seeing Walter there. Now I was caught in an impossible situation. I wanted to go hug my best friend who wanted to be my boyfriend and who I did not want to be my boyfriend. If I didn't, he'd be offended. With this added to the "talking to you is like talking to a girl" incident, he might never speak to me again.

But even more I wanted to keep hugging my partner who I wanted to be my boyfriend and who did not want to be my boyfriend. If I didn't . . .

Well, he didn't. Drew turned to see what I was looking at, then walked away from me without another word to me. As he passed Walter, he nodded and said evenly, "Walter."

Walter said, "General."

Drew punched Walter on the shoulder and kept walking.

"What's eating him?" Walter asked me, rubbing his shoulder. Then he hugged me. He'd missed me. I would have missed him, too, except that so much had been going on with band, and Drew.

I wanted to be happy to see Walter. But I felt slightly nauseated.

Which, I assured myself, was because I'd skipped lunch.

His beard tickled my cheek. I pushed him away. "What's with the scrub?"

He touched his chin. "At school they call me a good ol' boy because I'm from the country. I grew the beard to make a point. I'd wear overalls, too, but as you know, my wardrobe is somewhat limited."

"Speaking of which, new jeans?"

He stuck out his leg. "Thanks for noticing. Thrift store. New to me."

"What's the occasion? You *do* seem taller than the last time I saw you. Lots taller. Six inches taller."

"Six inches in two weeks? I think that would be painful." He still stared thoughtfully at his leg. I'd embarrassed him.

To change the subject, I asked, "What's in the box?" and realized too late that I didn't want to know.

"I brought something for you," he said. He showed me the clear plastic box with a homecoming corsage inside.

I peered at the chrysanthemum decorated in the school colors. It was no uglier than every other girl's homecoming corsage, but it looked unspeakably ugly to me.

Because when I put it on, it would

mean that I was on a date with Walter Lloyd.

"I figured you wouldn't mind," he said, "since we're already dating."

"*What?*"

"Yeah, I heard you couldn't go out with Barry Ekrivay because you and I are dating."

"Drew just blurted that out to Barry so I wouldn't have to go out with him."

The big green eyes stared hard at me. The beard made Walter look older after only two weeks. But he also seemed wiser, like the green eyes were seeing something in me they hadn't seen before.

Finally he said, "I'm glad Patton's so worried about your virtue."

"My virt— Walter, I challenge you to go two minutes without saying anything about sex. I'll bet you can't do it." I looked at my watch.

"Two whole minutes? If I can do it, what's the prize at the end? Can I choose?"

"That's pretty good. Five seconds." I looked back at the flower. "Walter, it's so sweet that you brought me a corsage." I meant to mean it. "But I can't wear it while I'm directing. It'll get in the way."

"Good point. It might not survive with you waving your arms around. We don't want you deflowering yourself all over the stadium."

I slapped him on the shoulder.

"Hey!" he yelled. "One drum major per shoulder. You take the left, and Patton can have the right."

"Walter," I said in a low voice. "Please don't call him that anymore. I'm trying to get along with him."

"Yes, your highness." He patted the box. "I'll just hold this for you."

"Good idea."

We walked around to the concession stand, got Cokes, and pushed our way up the stands to the band section. The drums crowded around him at one point, cheering, "He's back! Hey, bus boy!" Then Allison ran up squealing to hug him, but the majorettes distracted her. A football player's pants were torn, and they were trying to figure out whether his nice naked fanny was showing or whether he wore flesh-colored pads.

Mostly Walter and I were alone for the third quarter off. I didn't ask him why he hadn't e-mailed me. I hoped he hadn't really been that mad at me about our argument at the bus. I hoped he'd gotten busy with school and hadn't had time to write. I hoped he was getting involved with activities there, new friends, girls. Of course, if that had happened, he wouldn't have come home and half-asked me to homecoming without paying attention to my answer. I liked Walter so much—as a friend, hello!—and I hated the feeling that our friendship was about to fall backward off a cliff.

He told me he was amazed that the band, especially the drums, sounded so much better. I sketched for him why Drew and I had decided to get along. He didn't seem interested. He told me stories about the weirdo art school kids who smoked pot and wore black.

Drew stood near the aisle with his brothers. He was a little taller than either of them. They laughed with him and told him he'd done a great job. He kept glancing past them to me like he wanted to introduce me to Anthony and reintroduce me to Christopher, who probably never noticed me when I was a freshman and he was drum major.

I didn't know how to handle this. I couldn't tell Walter I wanted to leave him to meet Drew Morrow's brothers. Walter was only home for the weekend. Drew could have introduced me to his brothers at any time in the past month and a half that we'd been working together. It kind of irked me that Drew had suddenly decided I was worth knowing.

"Virginia," Drew called sharply.

I looked up. It was fourth quarter. Behind me, the band was back in place. Depending on whether the team scored, we might have to play the fight song at any second. I should have been watching the game, not chatting with Walter.

I was such a slacker drum major! I was glad I had Drew there to be alert for me. When he didn't have a fever.

"Virginia!" Drew stood in front of me, jaw clenched. He held out a hand to me.

"Cutting in?" Walter asked.

"Walter—," Drew started.

"Nnnn," I said, waving my hand between them. One could learn much from Mr. Rush. If one could stop oneself from saying "shit." I stood and let Drew pull me toward the aisle, away from Walter.

We faced the field so Drew could watch the game. Or so Walter couldn't see what we said. Drew put his arm around my waist so the band could see we were friends. Or so Walter would think we were more.

Drew said, "Walter has to go."

"But it's homecoming. And he's home."

"Virginia. Nobody in band gets to sit with their date during fourth quarter. That's why we get third quarter off."

"He's not my—" I stopped. I guessed Walter *was* my date. I wasn't sure. Technically, there had been no receipt of corsage.

I glanced behind me at Cacey up in the stands. Or the other one, whichever. She stared me down, trying to freeze me with her supervillain ice-vision.

She overflowed with corsage. This sucker was a huge chrysanthemum with all the bells and whistles—ribbons, golden plastic footballs, pipe cleaners shaped into the school letters.

I turned back to Drew. "Walter hasn't been gone that long. He's really still part of the band."

"Then he should be in his section, with the drums."

"He can't do that. He's not in band anymore."

"Then send him out. Don't try to argue logic backward and forward with me, Virginia. I just took the SAT."

He had me. And I'd had enough. "What do you care if he sits down here with me?"

"You know you wouldn't let Cacey sit down here with me."

"Of course I would. Let's call her down. Walter and I would enjoy the pleasure of her company."

Drew slipped his hand to my hip and bent his head closer to mine. "Look, Virginia. I'm discussing this with you calmly. I'm not stepping on your toes. I'm doing what I agreed to do in the meeting this afternoon with Mr. Rush. But in a minute, I'll start yelling."

"All right!" I yelled.

As I approached Walter, he stood. "Patton wants me out?"

I stopped myself from asking him again not to call Drew that. I was again beginning to think it fit. "Sorry," I said.

"You don't have to obey him, you know. You're drum major too."

"I told you. I'm trying to get along with him."

"I know you are."

"What's that supposed to mean?"

He shook his head and moved toward the student section across the aisle from the band. "I'll see you after."

I couldn't wait.

Fifteen

After the game Allison and I went home to change. Walter waited at Allison's house rather than mine because her parents liked him better.

This was perfect for my purposes. It made sense for the three of us to ride together to Barry Ekrivay's party a mile around the lakeshore. Otherwise, Allison would have taken her car, and Walter and I would have ridden together. Alone.

More good luck: When she got into the car, Allison sat on Walter's corsage. Now I wouldn't have to make a bad excuse about how wearing it would poke a hole in my T-shirt.

That's where my luck ran out. My heart

sank as I drove near Barry's house and saw how far away I'd have to park to get a place on the side of the road. I'd hoped it would be a small party, so fewer people would see me with Walter. But Barry didn't throw small parties.

With every step down the driveway, I felt more nauseated. But there was nothing else to do. I put a smile on my face before I walked into the house crowded with the entire band and lots more people from school.

I kept telling myself that no one would notice Walter and I were together. After all, I'd driven him to parties before. Nothing had changed. Let me repeat: There had been no official receipt of corsage.

Something *had* changed. Gator Smith stopped me and congratulated me on "finally hooking up." Then Tonya, Paula, and Michelle called me over and told me that Walter was "soooo cuuuuuuuuuute!" Oh, dear.

It wasn't that I was embarrassed to date Walter, himself. Tonya, Paula, and Michelle were right. He was very cute. And he was fun to watch as he walked around the party. He just laughed when the trombones quizzed him on his beard and the drums called him "bus boy." He was only a sophomore, but he carried himself well around the seniors. Which was better than *I* could do half the time.

It was more a feeling of complete revulsion. My head told me that Walter and I would make a good couple. Despite my head, my body flinched when he touched me. But maybe this was normal for new couples, and as time passed, people got over the vague feeling of nausea.

Like I knew!

And oh, let's not forget that I wanted to keep myself open for Drew. Who did not even seem to be at the party. Who must have been off having a private moment with Cacey.

I had a couple of tricks to keep the pressure off. I tried to get Allison to stay with Walter and me. Sometimes I lost Walter in the crowd. When he found me, I suggested that we also find Allison because she was there alone.

Allison flitted from group to group. I needed her to cling to me, and I tried to communicate this to her with special looks. But there's just so much you can get across with gritted teeth and a raised eyebrow, even to your best friend.

My other trick was to haunt the buffet. Yes, there was actually a catered buffet set up in the kitchen. Dad always said Mr. Ekrivay threw money at his children to make up for leaving their mother. I thought Dad had a lot of nerve to say this.

Anyway, the buffet was very good, and I'd skipped lunch. I'd eaten a huge supper, but I was trying to get away from Walter here. I went back so many times that Barry, who refilled the trays from boxes in the refrigerator, probably thought I was coming on to him.

On my seventeenth return to the rec room with my mouth full, Allison tried to tell me something. We were near the stereo speakers, and I couldn't hear her. I thought she said she was leaving.

Panic! She couldn't leave. What if Barry ran out of food?

She motioned toward the front door. I followed her out onto the porch. Walter followed me.

The huge porch was packed with outdoor furniture. The furniture was packed with people making out. I spotted Gator

Smith and Elke Villa, who I guess had settled whatever problems the Evil Twins had brought up between them.

Juliet Ekrivay was there too, with a senior football player. For *shame.* She was only in the ninth grade. But I'd had an unusually chaste ninth grade myself. And it was her porch.

"I'm leaving," Allison said.

"What?" I exclaimed in fake surprise. "Why so soon?"

"Nothing to keep me here." She wore the pageant smile, but I knew she was upset. She might have been the only homecoming queen in the history of football without a date to homecoming. I was impressed she'd lasted this long without a meltdown. As much as Allison ever had a meltdown.

I squinted to see what she was staring at in the dark. It took a minute for my eyes to adjust, but finally I saw the touch football game over on the lawn. Luther and Craig versus all eight girl trumpets.

"Take off your heels," I suggested. "I'm sure they'll let you play. You're Miss Homecoming."

"I hate this town," she said.

Now she was looking at the cars parked

in Barry's driveway. That's when I saw Drew. And Cacey. Leaning against the farm truck. Cacey lit a cigarette.

"At least they're not getting dirty with each other," Allison said. "He hasn't touched her hand." I'd told Allison about the whole hand-whore episode.

"What?" Walter asked.

"Inside joke," I said.

"But *I'm* on the inside," he said. "Aren't I?"

The three of us stood there awkwardly.

"So, I'm going home," Allison said. The pageant smile had returned.

"How?" Walter asked.

"I'll walk."

"It's dark," I said. "Call your dad to come get you." The more obvious plan would have been for me to take her home, but I was the Evil Triplet. My need to spy on my nonboyfriend overrode my desire to help my best friend.

She shrugged and said again, "I'll just walk."

"Let me take you," I said half-heartedly.

"Oh, no," she said, glancing over at Drew. "I don't think your work is done here."

If her comment offended Walter, he hid

it. He put his hand on her shoulder. "You want me to walk you?"

"Sweetie. No thanks."

I touched her elbow. "Call me to let me know you got there."

"No prob. Ta."

"Ta," Walter and I said.

We watched her walk up the driveway, past Drew and Cacey. Cacey was too into Drew to notice her sister's arch-rival. She eyed Drew and blew smoke out the side of her mouth, away from him, like an expert.

I wasn't sure, but it didn't seem smart to lean against a truck while smoking a cigarette. What if there was an explosion and Drew was blown to smithereens? Would Mr. Rush fire me and replace me with Clayton Porridge? Did he see Drew and me as a package?

I turned back to Walter. He was looking in the direction I'd been looking.

Better to admit it. "I was just thinking the Evil Twin might ignite the gas tank."

Walter watched Cacey and Drew for a few seconds more, then turned back to me without saying anything.

"You're out," I said.

"Of?"

"One-liners."

"Oh!" he said. "I thought you meant I was out of the picture."

"Thank goodness you're back," I said.

We laughed. Then his smile faded, and I felt mine disappearing too. We were talking about young love.

Weren't we?

I looked back to Drew. He was kissing the twin.

Ack, Drew was kissing the Evil Twin!

He had his hand on her waist. Unh, that was supposed to be my waist! He used his other hand to brace himself on the truck, and he bent to kiss her, a long hot kiss.

Well, it couldn't have been too hot a kiss, because she had the presence of mind to flick ash from her cigarette onto the driveway while it was going on.

I turned back to Walter. He was watching me.

Then I got an idea. It was the make-out porch. I could make out with Walter.

"Want to sit down?" I asked, nodding toward an empty——errr——love seat.

"Why not?" he asked.

I could think of a lot of reasons why not.

We sat close but not touching, and

joked quietly about the other couples making out. We rated them each with an artistic and a technical score. We did not rate Drew and Cacey.

I offered Walter all kinds of hints, but he wouldn't make a move on me. I sidled a little closer to him, so our knees touched, and gave him what I thought was a pointed look. I didn't want to make the first move. He was still crushing on me, and it would be cruel to lead him on.

But if he made the move on me, I could be nice and just enjoy it while we were in public, and then explain that I wasn't interested when we were alone. After I'd made my point to Drew.

The only problem with this plan was that Walter wouldn't cooperate. He wouldn't take the hint. Or he got the hint, but he was being stubborn for some reason.

I knocked my knee against his knee.

He looked down at our knees, but didn't otherwise move.

I reached out and touched his hand with one finger.

This time he looked up at me, and I knew for sure he was being stubborn. He was too smart for this. There was a reason he'd gotten into the State School for Fine Arts.

We stared at each other, and the air was electric between us.

My cell phone rang.

As I half-stood to pull it out of my pocket, I saw that Drew had turned toward me, with his arm still braced on the truck, very close to Cacey.

Allison was calling to tell me she'd gotten home okay. When I clicked the phone off, Walter asked, "Are you ready to go?"

I thought he knew I was crushing on Drew, and he knew I was only here to see Drew, and he knew he wasn't helping me give Drew the proper show. But I couldn't be sure.

Drew kissed Cacey's neck.

"Yes," I said.

Sixteen

I drove Walter across town. Neither of us said anything for the whole ride, which was probably the first time that had ever happened between us. Last year we couldn't even shut up when we were supposed to be standing at attention on the football field in the drum line.

I pulled my car into the campground and stopped at the door of the bus. His mother's car wasn't there, of course. The lights were off in the nearby trailers.

I was half-hoping he would jump out and go inside before I even turned off the motor, but I knew he wouldn't. Something was going to happen. I turned off the motor.

We sat there in the quiet dark. I stared

straight ahead at the bus. In the years since Walter had painted it brown, the paint had faded and cracked. The original yellow showed through.

The air around us began to spark again. We still weren't doing or saying anything, but that was the whole point. The quiet was so strange, and it said everything for us.

Finally, after about two minutes of complete silence, I looked at him. He was watching me. I stared back at him. Something would have to give.

I wondered why I didn't give. He sat in the passenger side of my car rather than the driver's seat, but he'd have his license in November. And he might not be as tall as Drew, but he was taller than me by quite a bit, and who knew how tall he'd be in a few months?

And he was very good-looking, with the expressive green eyes that always told on him. Now they were telling me that he had my number. He knew I'd tried to lead him on. He was mad about it. And he wasn't leaving this car until he got some. But he was going to make me wait.

I tapped my fingers on the steering wheel and wished I had my drumsticks.

Better to meet the problem head-on, right? Still tapping, I said, "At the party. On the porch. You knew what I wanted."

"Yes."

"And you wouldn't give it to me."

"No."

"Why not?"

"I didn't choose to help the cause."

"Fair enough," I said. Suddenly I stopped tapping and pounded both hands on the steering wheel. "I can't believe you're playing hard to get!"

"Me neither." He crossed his legs. "I'm afraid you're going to take advantage of me."

"I wouldn't *have* to if you would take advantage of me *first*!" Time to bring out the heavy artillery. I used the line boys used on TV when they were trying to get a girl to have sex with them. "You would if you loved me."

Of course I was kidding. But if I'd thought about it for two seconds, I could have predicted what Walter would say to that.

"I *do* love you."

The air between us sparked until I almost thought I could hear the tiny explosions.

"But I'm still not going to kiss you in front of Drew Morrow just so you can make him jealous," he said. "Or kiss you now because you're horny for Drew."

"Really?" I asked. "Then why are you still in the car?"

"Good point."

Walter would argue with me all night. Oh, what the hell. I leaned over and kissed him.

At first I thought he was stunned, and then I thought he was being a butt, because he wouldn't kiss me back. He didn't move. Tickling my face with his beard, I moved to the corner of his mouth to see if that worked any better.

Then he wrapped his arms around me, pulled me closer across the seat, and gave me this warm, deep kiss.

Walter was a great kisser. Not that I had a whole lot to go on. The last time I'd kissed a boy was at the movies in eighth grade. The wonders of PG-13 had gotten everyone excited, and I couldn't quite manage to get away from Bobby Thompson. After that, nothing for three years. The nose stud scared them off.

But even *I* could tell that Walter was

doing this right. There wasn't enough tongue to be gross, but just enough to wake me up. I mean, this boy was *waking me up*. It occurred to me that Drew wasn't the only playboy in the band. Walter had spent part of last year working his way along the clarinet line. It was paying off. For me.

This did not feel right. But it felt good.

I was giving Walter what he wanted. If his crush on me was anything like my crush on Drew, he'd probably dreamed for the past two years about kissing me. I was making my friend happy.

There was no way I could pull out now. Walter would hate me forever.

I could do this. I could do this for me and for Walter. I could pretend Walter was Drew.

His hand slid down my arm, and he interlaced his fingers with mine. His thumb rubbed my thumb.

I jerked away from him and backed across the seat, into the door.

He stared at me dumbly for a moment. "I knew it," he muttered. Then he shouted at me, "I *knew* it! This is why I went away to school!"

"No, it isn't," I said, trying to slow

down my panting. "You went away to school because you're a good musician and an incredible writer, and you wanted to get a better education. And running water."

He looked at the bus. "I'd drop out and come back in a heartbeat to be with you."

"I know. That's why it's called a crush. It weighs you down and keeps you from doing what you really want to do."

"What I really want to do is be with you."

Before I could stop him, he got out, closed the door, and walked toward the bus.

I was going to let him go. Anything else I did would just mess it up worse. But I finally opened my door and leaned out. "Walter," I called. "I don't want to leave it like this. I want us to stay friends."

He whirled around at the steps to the bus. "It's not all about you, Virginia. And sometimes you don't get what you want." He mounted the steps and slammed the door behind him. Which was difficult, because it was a folding door with a lever.

I waited for him to light a candle or a lantern in the bus. I watched from my car for a long time, but the bus stayed dark.

Seventeen

When I got home that night, Dad was at the hospital delivering a baby. It was Mom who was waiting for me, dozing on the couch with the Weather Channel on. I wondered why my parents had taken to watching the Weather Channel all of a sudden, like they were expecting a storm.

Mom was still in full makeup and looked like a magazine layout for expensive pjs, lying there in her negligee. Now, I don't mean to give the impression that my mother never got dressed. She didn't lie around in her negligee all day. Well, I guess she *did*, about two years ago. But she was depressed then, and it only lasted a week.

I lay down on the couch with my back to her front.

She stirred, pulled part of her silk robe over me, and kissed my hair. "You did so well today."

"Thanks."

"The band was night and day compared to two weeks ago. You've done a wonderful job with them. You and Drew. I'm so proud of you."

I tried not to shiver under her robe. "Thanks."

"And didn't Allison look glamorous in the parade?"

I looked down at Mom's hand resting beside mine. My fingernails were unpolished and cut down to the quick. Hers were long and red and freshly, professionally manicured.

"You know Allison has a big pageant tomorrow," I said.

"I know."

"Would you like to go?"

"Of course. I might go."

"I mean, would you like for you and me to go with Allison and her mom?" Before she got the wrong impression, I hurried on, "I don't think I'll ever do pageants again myself. I've had enough. But I want to support Allison. I feel bad that I haven't gone with her in the past two years. And the one tomorrow is so important."

"I think that would be fun," Mom said.

I fell asleep lying on the couch with her, wrapped in her silk, just like I used to.

And that's how I came to be riding back from Gadsden late Saturday evening with Mom, Allison's mom, Allison, and a pageant trophy the size of a refrigerator. It took up the whole payload section of the SUV and extended above the back seat, with the pageant girl on top poking between Mom and Allison's mom in the front.

When Allison's mom pulled into her driveway, I realized I didn't want the day to end. Allison had almost convinced me that Walter would get over our fight. It made me feel good to be around Allison, and I'd missed spending whole pageant days with her.

I glanced over at her. She looked so pretty. And very funny in a T-shirt, torn jeans, high heels, pageant makeup, pageant hair, and tiara.

We couldn't extract the tiara without washing her hair and starting all over again. She'd pulled out the majorette tiara before she went to Barry's party the night before, but that was majorette hair. Pageant hair was another animal. This was some high hair. You teased it and sprayed it until it was mostly air, with a shell of hair around it. The tiara was secured so tightly with pins and hairspray that it was practically glued in place.

Someone else should share this joke. It was a shame that no one from school ever saw her this way.

The pageant trophy was worth showing off too.

I had an idea. I never thought Allison would go along with it. And it wasn't long until our midnight curfew. But we dropped off our moms, borrowed Allison's mom's SUV still loaded with the trophy, and headed for Burger Bob's.

I'd had fun at the pageant. I was glad we'd all gone together, just like old times. But after twelve hours, *man*, what a relief to be rid of the moms! I rolled down my window—Allison couldn't roll hers down because the wind would destroy the hair helmet—and we cranked up the stereo. I pulled off the shoes my mom had made me wear inside the pageant showrooms. We sang along at the top of our lungs to songs on the radio.

After a few minutes Allison turned the volume down. "Serious convo for a minute."

Uh-oh, she was pulling at her earring. That meant it was *really* serious.

"No!" I turned the volume back up.

"Just for a minute." She turned the volume down. "I know you still care how you look. You haven't been wearing makeup, but you've been plucking your eyebrows, and I've seen the Proactiv in your bathroom. You go barefoot, but you're taking really good care of your toenails. And you're still using a pumice stone on that weird-looking place on your big toe."

I stuck out my tongue at her.

She went on, "When you stopped going to pageants, it was so sudden. And remember how hard we worked on your baton routine, and how happy we were when you made majorette? Overnight, you decided you didn't want to be a majorette anymore. It hurt my feelings. You know it hurt my feelings. You never hurt my feelings on purpose. Something happened to you."

I turned the radio volume back up.

She turned it back down. "Will you tell me someday?"

I said somberly, "Yes, I'll tell you someday."

She turned the radio up. I turned it back down. "By the way," I said, "while we're having serious convo. I'm glad you're going to Burger Bob's with me. I wish you would do stuff like this more often. I wish you wouldn't go around with your head in the clouds *all* the time."

"It's safer up here."

"I know. But Allison, you were really unhappy last night. I've never seen such an unhappy homecoming queen."

She pulled at her earring.

"I'm not saying you should come down to earth. If you're on cloud nine, I'm suggesting that you come down to cloud six, six and a half."

"Maybe," she said as she turned the SUV in at Burger Bob's.

She pulled into the front parking space,

nearest the road. This was the unofficial place where boys parked in the winter, during hunting season, and showed off the huge deer they'd killed in the woods that day.

She opened the hatchback, and both of us struggled to slide out the huge trophy and set it on the pavement. We sat on either side of the bumper.

Immediately people cruising from Burger Bob's to the movie theater and back honked their horns at us. Allison gave them her special pageant wave. And then someone hollered, "Hey, it's JonBenét!"

"Oh no," I said. I watched Luther's car turn off the street and into the Burger Bob's parking lot.

Allison laughed. "What do you mean, 'Oh no'?"

I looked at Allison like she was crazy. "Drew's here!"

"You knew you might see him tonight. That's the only reason I agreed to come here with you."

Before I could think of a comeback, Luther pulled his car into the parking space next to us. Luther, Barry, and Craig

Coley piled out of the car, crowded around us, and gave the trophy an "ooooooh, aaaaaah." Drew hung behind them, watching me.

"That's a big 'un," Luther told Allison in a dead-on redneck accent, which was hilarious coming out of this African-American guy.

"Reckon it is," Allison responded in a dead-on redneck accent of her own.

I turned to stare at her in amazement and new admiration.

"What'd you use to bag him?" Luther asked. "A twelve-gauge or a thirty-aught-six?"

"My feminine wiles," she said, batting her eyelashes. "And a thirty-aught-six."

He stepped closer to her. "I've been in class with you for eleven years, and I had no idea you had a sense of humor."

"Maybe I just don't laugh at your jokes. And maybe you're not as funny as you think." But she smiled at him. Not the pasted-on pageant smile, either. A genuine smile.

You go, girl. She was giving him the time of day. And he was giving it right back.

I boasted to the boys, "Today Allison was crowned Miss East-Central Alabama 2006."

The boys looked at me blankly.

"Now she gets to compete in the Miss State of Alabama pageant," I explained. "It's like shooting a fourteen-point buck."

"Oh," the boys said, nodding.

Barry and Craig tried to talk to me, but I babbled on. I was completely distracted. I was listening to the rest of Allison and Luther's conversation with one ear. Luther was saying something about knowing a good taxidermist. And I had one eye on Drew, who still shadowed Barry and Craig.

Suddenly, when I was in midsentence answering Barry's question about the food at his party, Drew reached between Barry and Craig, grabbed my wrist like he had that Friday night in the bathroom, and pulled me off the bumper.

I would have stopped him and jerked away, but it happened so fast. He opened the back door of Luther's car, shoved me in, scooted in next to me, and closed the door behind him.

It was that familiar feeling. I was in

the center of bustle, the traffic around Burger Bob's, but I was sealed off from the world. With Drew. I sat against the far door. He took up the rest of the seat, leaning so close to me that my skin tingled.

His low voice vibrated through me. "I'm sorry about that JonBenét comment. It wasn't me. It was Barry. He's still really interested in you."

I studied Drew, wondering what to make of this. Was Drew telling me Barry liked me because Drew didn't care? Or was Drew telling me because he did care, and he wanted to see my reaction? If this had been the eighth grade, I would have thrilled at playing mind games with a cute boy.

But I was tired of the mind games after last night with Walter. And this was not the eighth grade, and this was not just any cute boy. This was Drew.

He studied me right back. "You look like a different person. I didn't even recognize you. I saw Allison first."

He meant that I'd poofed my hair and applied full makeup this morning. "I was going to be around Allison and other pageant girls all day," I explained. "I didn't want to look like that purple-haired assistant next to Anna Nicole Smith."

"You couldn't look like that girl if you tried. And I think you've tried."

I grinned. "Remember this picture. You may never see it again. This is what eyeliner looks like when you put it on right."

He frowned.

I shouldn't have reminded him about the twin.

"You look beautiful," he said. "You always look beautiful. Are you dating Walter now?"

It took me a minute to catch up. I was still on "beautiful." *You always look beautiful.*

"What?" I said finally. "No, I'm not dating Walter. But we made out Friday night."

Drew's frown deepened. I thought he might be just a little bit jealous. Hooray!

But then he said, "I have a lot of respect for Walter. You've got to like a guy who takes living in a bus as well as he has. Don't play with him, okay? I can tell he really likes you."

I felt bad enough about Walter without Drew giving me a guilt trip. Who did he think he was, Match.com? "I wasn't playing with him," I said. "I was in the process of telling him that we should just be friends."

"Is that what you always do? Tell guys you want to just be friends with them, then make out with them?"

Well, I wasn't going to tell him that Walter Lloyd and Bobby Thompson were my entire experience. "Yes," I said, trying to sound offhanded. I glanced at the cars crawling in the drive-through lane. "Like takeout."

"Like a to-go box," Drew suggested.

"Exactly!"

"You told Mr. Rush in his office on Friday that you and I are just friends. And you didn't make out with *me.*"

"That would be because you're dating Miss Icktory's sister."

"No, I'm not. I broke up with her at Barry's party."

I tried not to laugh out loud. And failed. "I am so sorry!" I laughed. "Condolences. Why in the world did you break up with her?"

He laughed too. "She smokes."

"How do you know it's not Tracey who smokes?"

"They both smoke."

"Are you sure? Have you seen them both smoking at the same time, in the same room?"

"Yes. And anyway, I only started dating her because the entire senior class warned me not to. Then, after she or Tracey was evil to Allison, I didn't break up with her because everyone told me to—even though I should have. You know, I have a little problem with people telling me what to do."

"I hadn't noticed."

"But that wasn't fair to her, no matter how evil she or her sister is."

"I'm glad you're so worried about Cacey's and Walter's feelings," I said, patting his knee. "Very responsible of you."

"Well." He winced like he'd been punched. "Right after you and Walter left the party, Cacey let something slip about Allison."

I turned cold, just as I had in the school hallway outside the lunchroom the day before. "Something bad? Something racist?"

"I went home and took a shower."

Now *I* winced. Gazing at the traffic cruising the strip in front of Burger Bob's,

I couldn't imagine what it must be like to be Allison and to be stuck in this town until her graduation next June. I was her best friend, and I couldn't imagine.

Giggles broke through the silence. *Allison's* giggles. Luther sat on the tailgate with her, gesturing widely to the huge trophy like he was selling it on the Home Shopping Network.

Drew went on, "And I wondered why Cacey couldn't have said something a few hours before, so I could have broken up with her earlier." He still looked pained. "At Barry's party I was only hanging on to her long enough to make you mad. That's not very responsible. My punishment for all this was that I had to kiss her while she was smoking. The things I go through for you." He pinned me to the door with his dark eyes. "Did it work?"

"Of course not. Or if it did, I wouldn't admit it. You're not the least bit upset that I made out with Walter."

He frowned again. "I never thought you'd date Walter. You're too much alike."

I thought about this. Weird, but he was right. No wonder Walter made me nauseated.

What girl wanted to date herself? "Perspicacious," I said. "More perspicacious than me."

He put his warm hand on my shoulder, then moved it up to massage the back of my neck. Terrific. Now I would walk around with another phantom limb. Drew's head on my thigh. Drew's hand on my knee. Drew's thumb tracing my hand. Drew's hand on my neck.

"I feel happy," I said.

"I feel lust," he said.

Our eyes met. Then his gaze flicked down to my lips.

I giggled. *Stop giggling!* "I feel expectant."

"But I also feel curious," he said.

"I'll just bet you do."

He laughed. "No. I mean . . . You look so different." He touched his nose at the position of my nose stud. "Tell me what happened to you."

A wave of longing washed over me. I'd wanted to tell Allison in the car. I wanted to tell Drew. But I couldn't. "I can't."

"You can. I was about thirty seconds from breaking down in Mr. Rush's office. You know all of my secrets. And you managed to get out of there without telling us any of yours. Tell me what happened to you."

"I can't, Drew."

His warm hand moved up my neck to finger the hair at my nape. "Tell me," he said.

"My dad cheated on my mom."

His hand stopped on my neck.

I was stunned too that I'd said it.

"Your dad, Dr. Sauter?" he asked.

"Yes."

"Cheated on your mom, who made me breakfast?"

"More than two years ago."

Allison's laughter rang out. Over at the SUV Luther tapped on her hair helmet like he didn't believe real hair could be formed into that shape.

"You see why I can't tell anybody?" I asked. "My parents swore me to secrecy. It would ruin my dad's practice if anyone knew. Women would feel threatened. They want to imagine that their ob-gyn doesn't have sex. I can't even tell Allison. Especially not Allison, because our dads are partners."

His hand moved down my neck to my back and rubbed soothingly. It wasn't about lust anymore. It was about comfort. A friend comforting a friend.

I went on, "My mom did everything she was supposed to do to be attractive to a man. She was Miss State of Alabama 1982. She gave up her own education to help my dad get his education and a career. And in return, he cheated on her. And you . . . I don't know."

"I what?"

I was embarrassed to say it. I was afraid he wouldn't understand. But in the spirit of family counseling, I gave it a shot. "At the time, I sort of had a crush on you."

I cringed, waiting for him to laugh.

He didn't. His hand stopped on my back for a second, and then he started rubbing again.

I started again. "I mean, I was in ninth grade. Your brother was drum major. You were in the big bad tenth grade. You started the 'ooooooh, aaaaaah,' which I thought was pretty funny. I didn't really think you'd ask me out. But let's just say I put on my eyeliner in the morning with you in mind. And then you made that JonBenét comment. You made fun of me."

He said softly, "I didn't mean—"

"I know you didn't. And I know it had nothing to do with my parents. It was bad timing. The thing with my parents had just happened, and I made the connection. Why should I try to be what boys want when they make fun of me for trying? So I gave up and did what I wanted."

"Drums," he said.

"Yes."

"Nose stud." He touched the tip of my nose.

"Yes," I said.

He tapped my foot with his foot. "No shoes."

I wiggled my bare toes. "And I didn't want to be a majorette like Allison. I wanted to be drum major, like your brother. I didn't want to be the girl who glittered and danced in front of the band. I wanted to be the girl in charge of the band. Glittering will only get you so far."

I turned to face Drew because I wanted him to understand where I was coming from. "I was glad my parents stayed together. I was also so proud of Mom for nearly kicking Dad out. I didn't know she was that strong. But if she *had* kicked him out, what would she have done? She didn't finish college. She hasn't held a job in probably a quarter of a century."

"It's not like she'd be out on the street if she divorced your dad," Drew said. "She'd come away with something."

"A little Botox fund." I nodded. "But that's not much of a life."

"Some people would think that was a great life," Drew pointed out. "Just not you."

I shook my head. "Not me."

"You know," Drew said, "from the little I've seen, your mother's gotten over it."

I thought of my parents holding hands in the football stadium. "She has."

"So why aren't *you* over it?"

I sighed. "I don't know."

"I think I know." He slid one warm hand over my hands gripped together in my lap.

I stared down, not quite comprehending that his hand was on my hands. Very slowly a tingle crawled from my hands up my arms and shoulders and neck to my face, like sap rising in a tree in spring.

"I know how you feel," he said.

The tingle? No, parents. We were talking about parents. "You're kidding," I said. "Your dad cheated on your mom?"

"I have the opposite problem. My dad can't keep *off* my mom."

We laughed.

"No," he said, leaning forward so our foreheads almost touched. "I mean, I know that feeling. You argue with them, and you don't want to do what they tell you. But somewhere in the back of your mind you're thinking all along that they're perfect and they know best. You feel like you can be a kid and get in trouble, and in the end it will be okay because they've got your back." He picked up my hand and squeezed it. "And then they let you down."

"That's it," I said. "That's exactly it."

I stared at our hands. We were holding hands. I was holding hands in the back of a car with Drew Morrow.

And I was wearing a watch.

I jerked my hand away from Drew's and looked at the time. "Oh, God." I opened the door, stood up, and called over the roof of the car to Allison, "Hey, Cinderella. It's almost midnight."

Allison squealed. She directed Luther,

Barry, and Craig as they hefted the trophy back into the SUV.

Drew frowned up at me from inside Luther's car. "I wanted to talk some more."

"We have curfew," I said. I closed the door, rounded the car, and hopped into the SUV before he could even get out of the backseat.

In the rearview mirror I could see him watching us go. It probably wouldn't make sense to him, but suddenly I'd been very uncomfortable sitting so close to him in the back of the car. I'd said too much. Even to the crush of a lifetime.

Eighteen

By late Sunday afternoon the uncomfortable feeling had disappeared completely, and I needed a Drew fix. After he'd held my hand in Luther's car and come so close to kissing me—hadn't he?—I expected him to call or come over. He didn't.

I finally gave my mother clear instructions as to my whereabouts in the event that a tall, dark, handsome drum major happened by. Then I walked to Allison's.

Allison and I played Baton Battle at the end of her pier. In Baton Battle you throw the baton as high as you can, spin as many times as you can, and catch the baton. But you can't hit yourself or your opponent with said baton. And if you drop said baton in the lake, you have to go get it. The stakes were high because the past few nights, the temperature had dropped into the low 60s, and the water was cold.

We hadn't played Baton Battle in ages. We used to play it all the time (we were often bored as children). I wasn't doing well. I used to win more than half the time, but I was rusty, and Allison had been majoretting and performing her baton act in pageants.

And I was distracted. Every time the warm breeze swayed the trees, I imagined it was the *whoosh* of tires on the driveway. I fought the urge to rush to the front yard to greet Drew.

Allison got cocky. She picked up a second baton and twirled it at the same time she threw the first, turned around four times, and caught it.

She handed the batons to me. "I dare you."

"Do you want to stop this now and have a drum competition?"

"No."

With a sigh I twirled the first baton, threw the second, and turned. One turn, two turns, three—

"Hey, batter batter batter batter, swing!" a boy's voice called.

I heard a *plop*. Allison and I stood on the pier and watched the baton sink three feet to the muddy bottom of the shallows.

"What does this look like, Little League?" I asked Luther crabbily. I was wearing shorts, so I could wade in and kick the baton back to shore without getting my clothes wet. But I wasn't going to like it.

I was also annoyed at him because he wasn't Drew.

"I'll get it for you," Allison said. "Help me, Luther."

"That's not the procedure," I said.

She glared at me.

"Yes, please get it for me," I corrected myself. "I'm afraid of fish."

As she kicked off her high heels she instructed Luther on how to hold her under the arms and lower her into the lake. She planned to pick up the baton with her toes, and then he could lift her back out.

I hoped Luther could swim, because this maneuver looked precarious. I would feel even more annoyed if they both fell in and I had to save them.

But Allison brought the dripping

baton safely back onto the pier. She and Luther congratulated each other, and then—what the hell?—hugged each other. He sat her down and made a great show of patting her legs dry with the edge of his shirt.

"So, Virginia," he said. "What was up last night? You're off Walter Lloyd, and you've moved on to Barry?"

"No, I was never on Walter, and I haven't moved on to Barry."

"That's not what Drew thinks."

Allison raised her eyebrows at me.

I sat down on the pier with them. "It doesn't matter what Drew thinks, Luther. You're over here visiting Allison. Why isn't he over here visiting me?"

Luther glanced at Allison in embarrassment. Then he said, "Drew's on the tractor. He has to get the crops in or something."

"How rural," Allison said.

"You snob." He grabbed her with one arm around her waist and tickled her ribs.

She laughed like I'd never heard her laugh before. Her desperate cackles echoed across the lake and back. She braced her bare toes on the dock and tried to pull away from him. She didn't try quite hard enough.

"Time out!" I yelled into the giggle fit. "I would like more information on these crops."

Luther stopped tickling Allison. But he didn't remove his arm from around her waist. And she didn't make him. She settled back into him.

He turned to me again. "Drew's dad is working overtime at the mill to make extra money. Drew has to do the farm practically by himself. Haven't you noticed how tired he is? No, of course you wouldn't notice."

Allison slapped him playfully on the chest. "How ugly! What's that supposed to mean?"

"It means she's jumping from Drew to Walter to Barry."

"You are totally making up this thing with Barry," I said.

"Tell Drew that," he said. "After we left Burger Bob's last night, I thought he was going to kick Barry's ass."

"What!" I exclaimed. "Why?"

"Barry expressed his admiration for you, knowing Drew likes you too. As you found out in the lunchroom on Friday, you can only push Drew so far, and then . . ." He snapped his fingers.

Allison and I gaped at each other, and then at Luther.

Luther gazed down into Allison's eyes and smiled.

"And then *what*?" Allison insisted.

"Oh!" Luther said, like he'd completely forgotten what we were talking about. "And then Drew fell asleep in the back of the car. Like I said, he has to bring in the harvest. He stays exhausted."

"Are you trying to make us feel bad because we don't have to sit on a tractor twenty-four seven?" Allison asked.

"I don't see a whole lot of physical labor going on in your neighborhood."

"That's where you're wrong," Allison said triumphantly. "Virginia's dad makes her cut the grass." She turned to me. "Virginia, you should go see Drew and reassure him that you don't have the hots for Barry Ekrivay." She made a *go away* motion with her hand, like she was trying to get rid of me. Like she wanted to be alone with Luther. Like we were boy-crazy teenage girls.

Finally!

I followed Luther's directions to Drew's farm. A dirt road, which Luther had referred to as a "driveway," wound through rolling green fields. Dark green trees framed the fields far away, at the edges of the earth. A tiny white house and an enormous red barn crowned the biggest hill.

And then I saw the red tractor off in the fields, trailing a wake of dust.

Disappearing in a valley, then cresting the next hill.

Coming for me.

I parked my car under an ancient oak tree. Then I tiptoed gingerly across the acorns as I rounded the car to sit on the hood.

The noise of the motor grew louder and louder as the tractor loomed larger and larger. Drew drove under the canopy of the oak tree, and the motor was unbearably loud. Then he cut the engine. My ears rang in the silence.

The seat of the tractor was enclosed in a glass booth, but the windows were open. He slipped off his headphones and opened the door.

He was wearing worn, ripped jeans faded almost to white, and no shirt.

Yee-haw!

And he was filthy. Small pieces of straw

stuck to his tanned chest and hung in his black hair.

"I was just thinking about you," he said.

I grinned like an idiot. "What were you thinking?"

He pursed his lips. I *loved* that look he got when he was trying to keep from laughing. "That I wanted to spend the afternoon with you, but I'm stuck on a tractor."

"Very responsible of you," I said.

"And I feel stupid. I ran out of time last night. I forgot that you probably had a curfew."

I walked toward him, wincing as the acorns stuck to me feet. "I've never been this close to a tractor."

"Really? I feel like I've lived on it for the past month. I might forget and drive it to school one day. Want to go for a ride?"

He held out his hand to me. With one arm, he pulled me over the enormous tire and into the cab. He let me sit in the seat, and he stood beside me.

Then he opened a compartment below the controls and brought out a second set of headphones. He placed them gently over my ears, put his own pair back over his ears, and reached down to start the ignition.

"Wait," I said.

"What?" he asked, pulling his headphones off.

I pulled mine off. "You don't really expect me to drive this tractor while you hang on, do you? We'll be killed, and Clayton Porridge will be drum major for sure."

He looked around the tractor cab. "I don't want you to have to hang on. My dad would wring my neck."

"You drive, and let me sit in your lap."

He gave me a long look.

"Okay," he said in a friendly way, as if this were the most normal request in the world. I stood. He slid under me to sit down, and he patted his thigh. And I sat down in Drew Morrow's lap.

He slipped one arm around my waist. He reached with the other hand to start the tractor. As he leaned forward, his bare chest pressed against my back, and his chin rested on my shoulder. We were way past phantom limbs here.

We drove fast across the rolling hills, until we couldn't see the house and barn anymore, and there was nothing but the warm wind scented with hay, the green hills, and the deep blue sky.

"It's really loud," I said.

"What?" he shouted.

I shook my head. There was no way he could understand what I was saying over the noise of the motor, with headphones on.

After a while I murmured, "It's so beautiful out here."

"What?"

We went over a bump, and he tightened his arm around my waist to steady me.

I said, "I like your arm around my waist."

"What?"

He slowed the tractor to a stop down in a valley, in front of a pond that reflected the bright sun and the white clouds. We pulled our headphones off.

I repeated, "It's really loud, it's beautiful out here, I like your arm around my waist."

"Yes, yes, what?" He put his hand on my bare thigh.

I stopped breathing.

He slid his hand slowly down to my knee, and rubbed my knee gently with his fingertip. So weird how he could make me feel just by putting his hand on my skin.

He wasn't breathing either.

I said, "On the count of three, breathe. Onetwothree."

We both gasped.

I turned to look at him over my shoulder. My, but he was a beautiful boy. The sun made tiny rainbows at the edges of his dark hair and glinted white in his dark eyes.

He put his chin on my shoulder again and rubbed his cheek against mine. With his lips almost touching my lips, he whispered, "We should add this to the dip."

We both burst into a long fit of laughter. He held me tight with one arm so I wouldn't fall off his lap.

"Okay, okay," he said finally, still laughing. "Turn around." He put both hands on my waist and gently guided me until I was facing him, sitting on his leg.

"This is comfortable," I said.

He grinned.

"We could be an act at the tractor pull. The Morrow Family and Their Risqué Tractor Show."

He rubbed his thumb lightly across my lips. And then he kissed me.

Mmmmmmm, what a warm and lazy kiss. A perfect kiss for a Sunday afternoon in late September. On a farm.

Well, the kiss moved at a lazy pace. It was slow and thorough. But *I* did not feel the least bit lazy. Electricity zinged through me. I should have stopped him to make sure he hadn't parked the tractor on a downed power line. But I didn't.

After a long time he paused to spit out a fragment of hay. "I beg your pardon," he said.

"Certainly," I said, careful not to pant.

He kissed me. "Remember that night I had scarlet fever?"

"Mmmmmmm," I said. "Vaguely."

He kissed me. "Since then, all I've thought about is your hand in my hair."

"Mmmmmmm."

He kissed me. "Well, I was able to block it out during the SAT. But after that . . ." Kiss. "At first I thought it was the fever. The fever went away, but the feeling didn't."

I put my hand in his hair.

Honk! I pressed farther against him in alarm, then looked around at the steering wheel that one of us had just kneed or elbowed. "Why do you have a horn on a tractor?"

"Cows."

"Ah." I kissed him.

We made out on the tractor for a long

time, until the sun moved and changed color. I couldn't get enough of his mouth on my mouth, his kisses on my neck, his warm bare shoulders under my hands. What made it worse, or maybe better, was the feeling that it was too good to be true.

A high, muffled beeping played the first few bars of the opening song from our half-time show. Pulling his cell phone from his pocket, he winked at me. "Band geek."

He clicked the phone on. "Hello . . . Give me fifteen minutes." He eyed me. "Twenty." He pressed the button to hang up. "My mom."

"Where is she? Is she okay?"

"She's here. She's fine, but I have to go back to the house."

I looked at the sun, then at my watch. "I should get going."

He grabbed my hand. "Don't leave! It'll only take me a minute. She can't reach the Cheetos. Your dad says we're supposed to humor her."

"No, I really should go. I have a big algebra test tomorrow that I need to study for. I wasn't expecting this to happen."

"Me neither. I feel sorry for Walter."

I nodded sadly. Crushing on someone

who didn't like you back sucked royally. And up until a few hours before, I'd thought I knew exactly how Walter felt.

Drew squeezed my hand and let go. "I'm lucky you like me better. And I intend to keep it that way. Can you take a break from algebra? Can I call you tonight?"

"Yes. Can you take a break from fetching Cheetos?"

"She'll be through with Cheetos by then. After dinner she changes over to Ritz crackers with cream cheese and green pepper jelly. By bedtime it's ice cream."

He rubbed his hands up and down both my thighs, lighting them on fire. I didn't mind too much.

"We're close now, right?" he asked.

"I'd say so."

"And we can tell each other anything, right?"

"Right," I said warily.

"Have you been hiding my band shoes?"

Nineteen

I didn't see Drew at all after school that week. He spent the week on the tractor. He had to cut all the hay before a storm front came through on Friday. You can't bale hay when it's wet because it will rot. See, I'd learned something already! He was good for me.

He was really, really good for me. Each day, I saw him before school, at break, at lunch, and of course during band practice. And then, Friday in the lunchroom, we made a date.

He scooted his chair close to mine and bent to whisper in my ear. "Tonight after the game, will you come over to my house? And before you answer, let me just say that this is very important to me. I haven't kissed you since Sunday."

I considered my salad on the table. I was *not* going to miss another meal because of Drew Morrow. But the lunch period was half an hour long. I could flirt with Drew and still have time for salad. And Drew was so *delicious*.

"Why do you need me to come over?" I whispered back. "We already know what it's like to make out on a tractor."

"I also have a hay baler that needs testing," he said. "And an all-terrain vehicle. And a riding lawn mower. And a barn full of hay." He stroked his thumb up my thumb, then down into the hollow between my thumb and finger.

"Oh," I said. "In that case, I'd be happy to help you out." I shivered as his thumb made its way up to my fingertip and down the other side. "No PDA allowed in school."

"This isn't PDA. I'm hardly touching you." His thumb lingered and tickled between my fingers.

He really *was* hardly touching me. We weren't even holding hands, so we couldn't get in trouble. But I glanced nervously around the crowded lunchroom like we were doing something wicked.

"I'll bet you do this to all the girls," I said.

He shook his head and smiled. "I like your hands." He took my hand in both of his and ran his rough thumbs across it like he was reading my palm. "I used to watch you play drums when you were in ninth grade. That was amazing. You were really good, even back then. Fun to watch. You know, I called you JonBenét to get your attention, because I liked you. Stupid, I know. But your dad's job, and the money you've grown up with . . . It's intimidating when you live in an old farmhouse." He squeezed my hand. "I'm glad we've got that settled."

I made it a point not to swoon over boys. Note to self: Make exception for Drew.

I started and snatched my hand away at a clatter across from us, but it was only Allison setting down her tray. "Did you hear?" she asked.

"Hear what?" Drew asked.

Luther plopped his tray down next to Allison's. "I guess you heard."

"Heard what?" I asked, beginning to dread the answer.

Allison slid her eyes from me to Drew and back to me. She pulled at her earring. "Why haven't you heard this? Everyone in the school knows."

"That Virginia won drum major," Luther explained.

Allison gave Luther a *shut up* look, but Luther didn't understand it.

Luther went on, "And that Mr. O'Toole made Drew drum major too because he didn't think a girl could do it by herself. Allison, why do you keep kicking me? Ouch, you're wearing heels."

"It would have been better to tell them gently, when they were each alone," Allison said. "But I guess this is how boys do things."

"I don't know who you're calling a boy," Luther said.

I stared at Luther and Allison. I was still in Drew's barn, testing the freshly cut hay. I didn't want to leave the barn. My brain yelled to my heart, *Come out of the barn! Relationship over!*

Drew had been more interested in flirting with me than in eating when we first sat down, but suddenly he was hungry. He had a cheeseburger, fries, broccoli, and collard greens to get through before band practice. At the moment he was working hard on a salad with egg and bacon and something red on it. Beets.

"Who says I won drum major?" I asked without taking my eyes off Drew.

"The Evil Twins," Allison and Luther said together.

"No wonder!" I exclaimed, relieved, and almost angry that they'd bothered to tell me in the first place. "Of course it's not true. They're just mad that Drew broke up with Cacey. They're trying to stir up trouble."

"It's probably true," Drew corrected me between bites. "Their mother is the secretary of the Band Boosters, and she used to have Mr. and Mrs. O'Toole over to dinner a lot. Mr. O'Toole probably told their mother." He concentrated on his salad again.

Allison caught my eye. She understood that my expressionless drum major face was not going to last much longer before I started to cry right here in the lunchroom. "Drew, why are you acting like that?" she asked.

"Like what?" he asked with his mouth full.

"Why are you eating?"

"Lunchtime."

I shook my head at her. It was no use. But she held up her hand, signaling me to hold on. "Aren't you going to make sure Virginia knows that everything's okay between you two? It's not her fault that she won, or that Mr. O'Toole kept it a secret, or that the Evil Twins have told the secret now. It's not her fault."

"Back off," Drew said without looking up from his plate.

"What do you mean, back off? You've got a lot of nerve to——"

Luther put his hand on her shoulder. "Don't. You remember what happened the last time Drew told y'all to back off?"

"Right," Allison said, smiling tightly. "He's keeping everyone from trampling on his machismo, and you're letting him. Meanwhile, he's ruining his relationship with Virginia. Look at her."

I looked away, across the lunchroom, and noticed one twin or another staring at me with an evil grin. I turned back to Allison.

"He needs to reassure her that everything's okay between them," she said.

"Everything is *not* okay between them," Luther said. "Can you imagine how humiliating this is for Drew?"

"Humiliating!" Allison exclaimed.

"Yes, humiliating." Luther counted on his fingers. "He has to share drum major. With a girl. A *younger* girl. A rich, spoiled doctor's daughter. Who used to dress up like JonBenét Ramsey. And who's stopped wearing shoes. That was bad enough. And now, to top it off, he actually *lost* drum major to this person."

I wanted them to shut up. But I kept listening with a kind of horrified curiosity.

"Virginia is a good drum major," Allison said. "She wouldn't have won otherwise. If Drew feels humiliated, that's Drew's personal problem."

"Drew *would* have gotten over it," Luther said. "The trombones would still be badgering him about it, but if Mr. O'Toole had come clean and told Drew he lost the election in the first place, he would have gotten over it." He shrugged. "But now Drew's spent a couple of months going through the motions, thinking he won, and thinking Mr. O'Toole gave Virginia the position because he had a thing for little blondes. It's completely humiliating for Drew to find out that he didn't win after all, and he's just a charity case. Now he has to quit."

"Quit!" Allison squealed. "He can't quit!"

"The position is rightfully Virginia's," Luther said. "He *has* to quit. Otherwise, his dad will kill him. His dad will kill him anyway for losing."

"But what about Drew and Virginia's relationship?" Allison insisted.

Drew was still eating. Holding my breath, I waited for Luther's verdict on our relationship.

"What relationship?" he asked. "It hasn't even been a week. They've made out once, and they haven't been on a date yet."

"But they've been leading up to this for months."

"Well, it's over now," Luther said. "I'm sorry, but Drew can't get past this. It's not just him, do you understand? It's his dad and his brothers who think he's let them down. It's the trombones and the whole school laughing at him."

"If he really liked her, he would be big enough to get past it." Allison stood up, teary-eyed. "I can't believe I trusted you! I thought you truly liked me, or I wouldn't have hooked up with you. But clearly, you'll take whatever you can get, wherever you can get it, and I was your latest target!" She whirled around and stamped daintily away.

Luther watched her go. "What just happened?"

I said quietly, "Girls are shocked when they find out how boys really think."

He looked at me in alarm, scraped back his chair, and ran after Allison.

Drew had started on his cheeseburger.

"We don't even know for sure that the rumor is true," I said. "I'll go ask Mr. Rush."

"You do that," Drew said.

At least this was probably the last lunch I would skip for Drew's sake. I raked back my chair and turned for the door, but a lunchroom lady stood guard. I grabbed up my full tray from beside Drew and took it to the dishwasher. As I passed, people at the tables on either side of me bent their heads to whisper.

Twenty

I opened my umbrella against the soft rain outside, but I took off my flip-flops so I could feel the cold, wet grass between my toes. And when I hauled open the band room door, my wet foot slipped on the cold tile. I landed with a *splat* on the floor.

Mr. Rush leaned out his office door. "That sounded like you. I've been expecting you. Where's the other one?"

I picked myself up off the floor. Shaking my head, I walked into Mr. Rush's office and closed the door behind me.

He stared at the door for a moment like he would get up and open it. Then he gave in and looked at me expectantly.

"How long have you known?" I asked.

"Since I got the job."

I took a deep breath and let it out slowly, like Drew did, with the self-control of an authority figure. "I feel . . . betrayed."

Mr. Rush nodded.

The self-control thing didn't work for me. "Why didn't you *do* something?" I asked desperately.

"I called my advisor from college. She told me if it ain't broke, don't fix it."

"It was clearly broken."

"I didn't think so at first. I thought you were two nice, trustworthy kids who hadn't been trusted. You were both good drum majors. You were into each other. I thought you could work it out. If I could find out what was behind Morrow's steely exterior. And your nose stud. But maybe you're right."

I held out a little hope, though I wasn't sure what I hoped for. "When you got the job, did you count the votes again?"

"Yes."

"How many did I get?"

He shrugged. "I don't remember. Seventy-something."

"How many did Drew get?"

"Three fewer than you."

I could tell by the way my heart sank that I'd hoped I had lost. To keep up the image that I was just checking his math, I asked, "How many did Clayton Porridge get?"

"Two."

I swallowed. "I think Drew may quit."

Mr. Rush nodded again. "I think you're right."

"We've gone all this time with Drew as drum major. We have a game tonight and the contest tomorrow. Drew should stay drum major with me."

"I agree."

"But he's humiliated," I said. "And he thinks the job is rightfully mine. He won't do it."

"No, he won't."

I closed my eyes, breathed the humid air, and listened to the noise outside the office. We couldn't practice on the football field in the rain. People hauled their instruments out of cases into the band room.

The familiar sounds of clarinets warming up and boys laughing should have been comforting. My whole life hadn't changed. Just this one thing. Really, everything was back to normal, with Drew hating my guts.

It was the past few weeks that had been unusual.

I *knew* the tractor love was too good to be true.

I opened my eyes. "And I bet you plan to drop another bombshell at the faculty meeting this afternoon."

"I can cause us trouble without even going to a faculty meeting," Mr. Rush said proudly. "For the contest tomorrow, I entered us two classes up from where we should be for the size of the school."

"So we'll be competing with all the huge, rich bands from Birmingham and Montgomery. *Why did you do that?*"

"It'll look so much more impressive when we beat the pants off them. I'll get my contract renewed for sure."

"Except that we won't beat the pants off them with Drew gone," I pointed out.

"There's that. I entered us two classes up before I knew this secret had gotten out." He winked. "No pressure."

Frustrated, I stood and jerked the door open, hoping I might find some snooping flutes to vent my anger on.

No one was there but Drew, leaning against the wall with his arms folded.

His dark eyes stared right through me, chilling me down to the bone.

He didn't say a word as he brushed past me into Mr. Rush's office and closed the door.

Immediately Mr. Rush opened the door again. "Sauter, go take roll and tune them up. I may be a minute." He closed himself in the office with Drew.

I stood on the podium in the band room and called names. Cacey and then Tracey Reardon answered after a long pause. I never looked up from the roll book. I was more interested in the voices of Drew and Mr. Rush that sometimes reached me through the closed office door.

I dragged the roll out as long as I could, then directed the band to play a note and hold it. Under the clean clarinets and the rich mellophones, I thought I heard an off-key flute.

But it didn't matter, because people stopped playing and strained to hear what Drew shouted at Mr. Rush.

The door to Mr. Rush's office crashed open and Drew stormed across the band room. The heavy door out to the driveway slammed behind him.

Mr. Rush walked into the band room and up to the podium. Everyone watched us.

"Where's Drew?" I whispered.

"I sent him to run laps around the football field."

"In the rain?"

"It's good for him." He turned to the band and yelled, "Holy crap, is it stuffy in here? Washington, open some windows."

Luther dutifully weaved between the rows of chairs, stood precariously on a tuba case, and cranked open the windows high in the wall. Girls in the back row squealed as rain blew in and wet them.

Mr. Rush handed me a sheet from a yellow pad. "Here's a list of trouble spots in the music that you need to rehearse them on."

"Me? What are *you* going to do?"

"I'm going to play drums."

"You flunked percussion."

"I know. I need to improve. Whoever heard of a band director who can't play drums?"

I had just become the lone drum major. The last thing I needed was to be put in charge! Reluctantly, I finished tuning the band and started rehearsal.

But at least with Mr. Rush in the

drum section, the left half of the room behaved themselves for fear of pissing him off. That included the twins and their flute friends.

The trombones were another story. The talking and cutting up slowly welled until I turned to them with my hands on my hips and sent them an outraged glare. They would titter and shush themselves. Then the talking would well up again.

I knew what was going on. They were angry with me about Drew. They were showing their loyalty to Drew by giving me a hard time.

And Mr. Rush was letting them do it. He was giving me a trial by fire.

Thunder boomed too close, and the lights flickered.

Girls screamed.

The heavy band room door banged open, and there were several more slams in the storage room. Drew appeared with his trombone, kicked Luther's chair so that all the trombones moved down one chair, and sat without saying anything to anyone. As if no one would notice him.

He was completely soaked.

Luther slid toward Barry to avoid getting dripped on.

I restarted rehearsal. The noise in the trombone section grew again, and expanded to the trumpets. I let it go on for a few minutes. It was only natural for them to talk. A down-and-out Drew was something to gossip about.

The noise expanded to the saxophones. I could hardly hear the flutes I directed. Then, from somewhere low in the trombones, an "ooooooh, aaaaaah" boiled up.

"Trombones," I called.

Drew leaned over Luther, talking to trombones farther down the line.

That was the last straw.

"Hello, trombones!" I yelled. "Drew!"

Drew's head snapped up in surprise, scattering raindrops. His eyes were wide, and a blush crept into his cheeks.

He'd been trying to get the trombones to shut up. He'd been discussing the problem with them. For me. He felt hurt.

I didn't care. I felt abandoned.

"It doesn't matter what's happened today," I said to Drew. Then I let my glance fall across the rest of the band, as if I were talking to them. "We still have a game tonight and a contest tomorrow."

I let the uncomfortable silence settle. If another "ooooooh, aaaaaah" broke out, I would throw up.

But it didn't.

At the back of the band, where no one else could see, Mr. Rush gave me a thumbs-up.

Any other time I would have felt proud of myself for handling the band and finishing what turned out to be a pretty productive rehearsal. I smoothed out all the rough spots on Mr. Rush's list, plus some I'd heard myself or that Drew had pointed out to me before. I thought we would sound a lot better after this.

But under the circumstances, I just wanted to get through it and go home and hide.

Which I did. For about an hour. Then I had to come right back to school to pile onto the bus for the away game in Birmingham.

As we stood outside the waiting buses, Allison gave me one last supportive hug underneath her umbrella. Then she got onto the senior bus. Drew was already on it in his regular band uniform, I guessed. I walked alone through the rain to the freshman bus. It didn't matter how wet I got. I couldn't use an umbrella at the game, anyway. Drum majors had more important things to worry about.

I took roll, made my way down the aisle over coolers and uniform bags, and sat in the backseat, reviewing the changes I would have to make in the halftime show now that Drew was gone. I closed my eyes so I couldn't see the curious looks from the freshmen or the concerned look from Ariel and Juliet across the aisle.

"Virginia," someone called. Then a chorus of voices: "Virginia, Virginia."

I squeezed my eyes more tightly shut. I hated band.

"Virginia." I recognized Allison's voice. She stood at the front of the bus.

I wove back up the aisle and followed her down the stairs, into the soupy grass.

"The twins are spreading another rumor about you," she said. She pulled at her earring.

She held her umbrella over us, but even out of the rain, the air practically dripped humidity. This afternoon, in the hour we'd had at home, I'd curled her hair carefully around her tiara while she chatted about whether Luther liked her bangs down or away from her face. If she was braving the elements to tell me about a rumor, it was bad, bad, bad.

"How bad can it be?" I asked.

"Did your dad have an affair?"

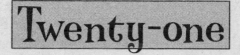

Twenty-one

By kickoff time the rain had stopped. First quarter, our team made a touchdown and two field goals. I sat at the bottom of the stands with my back to the band, watching the game closely. I was terrified I'd miss when we were supposed to play the fight song.

Conveniently, while I was watching the game, I didn't have to look at the twins, who had told everyone about the drum major fiasco. Or at Drew, who had told the twins about my dad.

Second quarter, our team made a touchdown and a field goal. I realized there was a pattern to the way the teams threw and kicked and ran. Almost like a game. A cold mist began to fall.

I was supposed to lead the band toward the field for the halftime show at the six-minute marker. As the time ticked down, I watched the clock, and then the game. The clock, then the game. Then Walter.

Walter passed in front of the chain-link fence that separated the band section from the lower section of bleachers. His beard was fuller now. I wouldn't have recognized him except for the way he walked, and then I caught a glimpse of his big green eyes. He was with a girl wearing black. Another girl wearing black and a boy with a long ponytail followed close behind them.

Walter dropped the girl's hand, stared straight at me, and held both arms up. He mouthed, "Touchdown."

What? Walter was *sexually active?*

"Drum major!" the band called behind me.

Oh, *that* kind of touchdown. I turned around casually and directed the band, as if I meant all along for there to be a time delay between the team scoring and the band playing the fight song.

As soon as the song was over, before Drew or a twin or anybody could even put their instrument down and catch me with their evil eye, I whirled back around.

Walter had his hand cupped to his girlfriend's ear. His friends moved down into the lower stands without him. He stepped closer to me and put his hands on the fence between us.

I put one hand up to touch his. But I watched the game over his shoulder. "Thank you," I whispered. I wanted to tell him so much more. How grateful I was that he would hitch a ride across Birmingham and drag his cool friends to his country high school football game to see me. If this whole horrible experience had taught me nothing else, at least now I knew who my friends were.

Of course, he might have brought his girlfriend just to make me jealous. But that's not how it felt when our fingertips touched.

"What happened to Patton?" he asked.

Forget the emotionless drum major face. I screwed my eyes shut to keep the tears away.

"Okay, okay," he said soothingly. "Watch the game. I'll call you tomorrow. You still have a contest tomorrow?"

I nodded.

"I'll call you tomorrow morning." We couldn't squeeze our hands through the fence, so we just did a pinky-swear, and laughed. And then he was gone.

The clock read six minutes, and I motioned for the band to follow me. Thank God I didn't have to keep up with the game for the next six minutes.

By halftime the mist had turned to drizzle. The dip did not work so well with only one drum major. It took two to tango. I did the military salute Drew and I did the first game, back when we weren't speaking to each other.

I held the salute, blinking the raindrops away, until the announcer had run through all the band officers' names. Mr. Rush had forgotten to change the list. "Drum majors," the announcer called. "Drew Morrow and Virginia Sauter."

My mother waved frantically to me from the stands. She blew me a kiss in support, then took my dad's hand again under their umbrella. During the brief time I was home after school, I'd told them Drew quit. I hadn't gotten into why, because I didn't want to break down. And of course they didn't know about the other rumor.

Yet.

I thought the show sounded good. I couldn't be sure. I had to pay close attention to what I was doing. There were a hundred little differences that I needed to remember now that I was covering Drew's job as well as mine. It would be like me to turn the band to the left when I meant the right.

Drew would love that. And there was no way I would give him the satisfaction.

Though it really didn't make any sense for Drew to have betrayed me. I'd pondered it for the whole bus trip. The more I considered it, the less sense it made. Drew wasn't vindictive. Impatient, yes. Hotheaded, yes. Vindictive, no.

Then again, when my dad cheated on my mom, she never saw it coming, because it didn't seem like him.

My mom had forgiven my dad. I wasn't ready to forgive Drew.

But my dad had asked to be forgiven. Drew apparently couldn't care less.

By third quarter the drizzle had turned to a deluge, and the band dashed under the bleachers. I'm sure Mr. Rush would have made us stick it out, except that some instruments like flutes and clarinets would be ruined if they got too wet.

I wished he would let us give up and go home. But he seemed to think that the rain would stop and we would go back to the stands to play some more. Anyway, we had to wait for the rain to let up just to get the flutes and clarinets back to the U-Haul.

Under cover of the bleachers, I walked toward a cluster of majorettes. I had been able to deal with the rumors while I had a job to distract me and I had my back turned to the stares and the whispers. Now that I was exposed in the middle of the band, I wanted Allison for support.

Drew watched me as I passed. He said something to the trombones grouped around him, and they all turned to stare at me too. Why they didn't go ahead and give me a big "ooooooh, aaaaaah," I didn't know.

One of the twins and her friends sat near the trombones, against the cement block wall of the concession stand. They mumbled my name, and something about my boots.

I walked over and stood very close to the

twin, so my boot almost touched her band pants. I looked down at her. "Why don't you stand up and say it to my face?"

She gaped up at me, clearly shocked that someone would call her on her evilness.

"That's what I thought," I said. I turned to find Allison.

There was a commotion behind me. The twin had gotten up to kill me.

Instantly there were trombones surrounding her, preventing her from clawing me. All she could do was shriek at me.

Drew had me by the wrist. He pulled me a few paces, then backed me against the cement wall. "You're drum major," he whispered hoarsely. "You can't stoop to that level."

I looked up into his beautiful dark eyes. "You would know."

He gave me the hurt look again, like I'd wronged him instead of the other way around.

That just made me angrier. "You've got a lot of nerve," I went on. "Don't you *dare* give me any more pointers."

I pulled away from him.

I could still feel the tingle of his hand on my wrist. Just what I needed.

I walked over to Mr. Rush. He didn't look particularly absorbed in his conversation with Mr. Scott, the biology teacher. Apparently Ms. Martineaux couldn't handle being a band chaperone. Or Mr. Rush's date. Mr. Scott was her replacement on the senior bus.

"Holding up okay?" Mr. Rush asked me. "I knew you would." Apparently he hadn't witnessed the scene of evil.

"Yes. But I'm taking ten." I gestured to the band. "Can you handle this while I'm gone?"

"I'll do my best."

Grabbing Allison as I passed the majorettes and dragging her with me, I stalked across the cement. My expressionless drum major face held until Allison and I got inside the door of the empty restroom. Then I started bawling.

I was short and she was model-tall. She held me tightly while I cried into her chest and told her the whole story. If she was miffed at me for spilling the beans to Drew and not her, she didn't mention it. Maybe she understood why her parents couldn't know. Or maybe she figured I'd suffered enough. It was a good thing tears didn't stain sequins.

After a long time I straightened, and she let me go. "I thought I wanted to be drum major by myself," I sobbed. "I got what I wanted. And I'm back where I started, crying in the restroom. With you."

"Yes," Allison said somberly, "but in the meantime, we've grown closer."

I snorted, and started to laugh, and choked myself.

She was pounding me on the back when someone knocked on the restroom door.

"Yes?" Allison called.

The door opened a crack, and Luther's voice echoed through the room. "Virginia, Drew wasn't trying to cause trouble in band practice today. He was trying to get the other trombones to lay off you."

Allison crossed the room and swung the door wide open. "You go back and tell Drew Morrow that's the least of his problems." She closed the door in Luther's face. As an afterthought, she opened the door again. "Are you still coming over after the game?"

"Yes," he said.

"Good." She closed the door in his face again. Then she wet her hands in the sink and began to pat the hissy fit off my skin.

"Maybe you should forgive him," she said.

I sniffed. "He hasn't asked me to forgive him."

"He probably will, if he already sent Luther in here to grovel to you."

"I can't believe he did it," I said. "I just can't believe Drew did this to me."

Allison shook her head. "Me neither. He was really mad. He wasn't thinking."

"Yes, he *was* thinking. He must have been thinking. Of all the things he could have done to get back at me, he picked the one thing that hurt most." I sniffed gigantically. "But I'm almost glad it happened."

She stopped blotting under my eyes with a paper towel and looked at me. "This should be good."

I explained, "I was tempted to tell you about my dad when we drove to Burger Bob's last weekend. I told Drew instead, while you and Luther were trading hunting stories. I was so relieved to finally tell somebody."

"To get it off your chest," she said, nodding. "It was a big burden."

"Partly that. But honestly, Allison, I

think part of it was getting even with my parents. And now I'm upset that I may have ruined my parents' lives, but I'm a lot more upset about losing my boyfriend of six days." I sighed. "I don't want to be a troubled teen."

"You're a long way from troubled teendom. You haven't broken any laws."

"I have a nose stud."

"That's an enhancement of your natural beauty," she said. "In some cultures."

I crossed my arms and hugged myself. "I cringe every time I look at my dad."

She rubbed my back. "I know."

"And I don't think it has to be that way. After Drew and I had that fight in the lunchroom on homecoming day, Mr. Rush made us go through family counseling in his office. You share your feelings, and the other person can't interrupt. You have to listen to each other. You communicate."

Allison stared at me dubiously. "Yes, I can see how your relationship with Drew is so much better now."

"It *is*," I insisted. "It *was*, until I found out that he's a rat bastard. We have the contest tomorrow, but Dad's off the whole weekend. On Sunday I'm going to sit him down and tell him how I feel. Maybe Mom, too."

"Are you going to tell him what you did?"

I laughed. "Remember how Drew told Mr. Rush I'd slept with Mr. O'Toole? And Mr. Rush said, 'What do you think you're doing? Tattling on her for having sex with a teacher?'"

Allison laughed too. "You sound just like Mr. Rush. That's scary."

I could think of worse things to sound like. Mr. Rush had been scary at first, but he was a lot more perspicacious than he let on.

"It's the same thing with my parents," I said. "What are they going to do? Ground me for telling someone that my dad had an affair?"

Allison raised one perfectly shaped eyebrow. "I see your point."

"Anyway," I went on, "I want to tell him what I did. He told me what he did. I see now that he didn't have to tell me, or even Mom. He probably could have hidden that it ever happened, but he decided to be honest. I need to give him the same respect."

Another knock sounded at the door.

"What!" Allison protested.

Mr. Rush swung the door open. "Sauter," he barked. "Time to march back to the buses. Either come be a drum major or let me borrow your skirt."

Twenty-two

As I walked toward the freshman bus I could hear them through the open windows. Girls screamed, "Eeeeeew!" as boys threw sopping wet items of clothing. I did not look forward to an hour and a half of riding home with these people.

Alone.

At the same time, I wanted to get on the bus as quickly as possible, to escape the terrible sight in front of me. The bus was parked next to the U-Haul. Instrument cases were being tossed, hauled, and slung along a line of boys.

Including Drew.

In a soaked T-shirt that stuck to his strong chest.

Rat bastard.

Mr. Rush sat on the bus stairs. He looked wet and tired, like a small, ferocious dog who'd been into the pond after a tennis ball one too many times. I started to climb past him into the bus, but he patted the stair beside him. "Sauter. Sit a spell."

I sat down next to him with a *squelsh* of water in my boots. "I don't want to let you down tomorrow."

"I don't want you to let me down either. I don't expect you to. You're doing a great job, Sauter. True, it would be better to have Morrow. Lots better. The whole thing, the whole band is planned around Morrow being there. It's Morrow who's letting me down." He lowered his voice. "Tell me what's been going on."

"How much have you heard?" I asked.

"I heard about your dad."

Drew handed a tuba case off to the next boy in the line. His eyes met mine for the briefest moment, and then he reached out for a drum case.

"Good news travels fast," I said.

"Clarinets know all and tell all," Mr. Rush said.

"Did you hear that Drew's the one who told the twins, who told everybody?"

Mr. Rush turned and looked at me. "What? Because he was mad about this whole drum major election hullabaloo? That doesn't sound like Morrow."

"It had to be him. I didn't tell anybody else." I shifted uncomfortably on the step, and water squished between my toes inside my boots. "Drew knows the twins have it in for me. When he told them, he *knew* they'd tell. But when I told Drew, I trusted him. I *trusted* him, you know? Like my dad trusted me when he told me in the first place."

Mr. Rush didn't say anything. We both watched the boys methodically tossing the black cases along the line. But I took his silence to mean that he was waiting for me to hear how I sounded.

"That's the thing, isn't it?" I asked. "Maybe I *shouldn't* be mad at Drew. Maybe I *am* just mad at myself."

"Don't be so hard on yourself, Sauter," Mr. Rush said. "It all goes back to your dad, doesn't it? He did the deed. And he told you. He's been sixteen. Or however old you were when this happened."

"Fourteen."

"Your dad's been fourteen. He'd be a real dumbass if he thought a fourteen-year-old could take a secret like that to the grave. Is your dad a dumbass?"

"No," I said.

"So he must have known you might tell. But he wanted you to know, and he would suffer the consequences. That's the kind of person he is."

And I'd wanted Drew to know. And now I was suffering the consequences too.

"Drew clearly is not into me like you thought," I said bitterly. "What's sad is, knowing that, and knowing what he did, I'm still into him. Isn't that the stupidest thing you ever heard?"

"Yes," Mr. Rush said. "Stupid and human."

We looked at each other.

He was thinking about Ms. Martineaux.

We understood each other.

He went on, "Drew lights a fire under you. He's responsible, like your dad wasn't. At least, you *thought* he was responsible. Now you can't quite believe what he's done. But when you believe it, the fire will go out.

"You light a fire under Drew because you know who you are. That's something he wants so badly for himself, but he's got too many people pulling him in different directions. If it's any consolation, a long time after your fire goes out, he'll still be burning for you. Trust me."

I remembered what Drew said when Barry asked me out: *One underhanded trick deserves another.* I could spread a rumor about him like he'd spread one about me. I could tell everyone not to trust him because he told my secret. But that wasn't my style.

And I couldn't even be consoled by the idea that he might crush on me after I'd forgotten him. The thought just made me sad. It made me want to put my arms around him. Awwwwww.

How sick was *that*?

Well, Mr. Rush was trying to help. I could return the favor. "Can't you tone it down for Ms. Martineaux?" I asked.

He looked at me like I was from Venus. "What?"

"When I've seen you with Ms. Martineaux, you've talked to her straight just like you talk to me and Drew." I glanced sideways at him. "Not that there's anything wrong with that. But if the way you're coming off is driving people away, maybe you should change."

"If she can't stand the heat, she needs to stay out of the kitchen," Mr. Rush insisted.

"Or you could air-condition the kitchen," I said. "Or at least install a fan to ventilate some of the fumes."

He chuckled, and gave me the first genuine, nonsarcastic, nonthreatening smile I'd ever seen on his face. "Get some sleep tonight." He pushed off from the bus stair and headed toward the other buses without concern, like it wasn't raining.

"Mr. Rush?"

He turned around.

"Thanks for telling me about that 'I feel' stuff. I think I'm going to do it on Sunday with my parents. I'm tired of being a troubled teen."

He laughed. He guffawed. He bent over and held his sides. I thought he was going to bust a gut right there in the rain. The line of boys stopped passing instrument cases into the U-Haul and stared at him.

Except Drew, who stared at me.

Mr. Rush wiped his eyes. Which seemed kind of pointless, since he was standing in a downpour. "Oh, Sauter," he said. "You're not a troubled teen. I know 'em when I see 'em. I was a troubled teen myself not too long ago." He turned and walked toward the other buses again. Then he tossed over his shoulder at me, "I spent some time in juvy."

Twenty-three

Allison and I were sitting in my car the next morning, watching the first bus park outside the band room for the trip to the contest in Montgomery, when my cell phone rang.

We looked at each other.

"Drew?" she asked.

I handed her my phone and the keys and got out of the car. When Luther came over to her house the night before, she told him that Drew had spilled the beans to the twins. Luther said it didn't sound like Drew, and he planned to call Drew and ask. That's probably why Drew was calling me now.

But if Drew wanted to be forgiven, I

still didn't want to hear it. And even if I eventually forgave him, I wasn't sure I could ever take him up on his offer to make out on a hay baler.

I chose a sunny spot on the wall near the band room door and watched the second bus pull up. After Luther had left the night before, Allison had come over to my house. We had stayed up late, blotting our soaked boots and band outfits and very carefully blowing them with hairdryers so they wouldn't shrink. My jacket and skirt and knee-high boots were warm and dry. And the stormy front had blown through, taking the cold rain with it, and leaving behind the warm morning sun.

But I couldn't shake the chill.

The saddest thing was that despite everything, I wanted to sit in this sunny spot and watch Drew drive up in the farm truck and climb onto the senior bus. Just because.

It was actually kind of strange that he wasn't there yet. He usually was way early because he was so responsible.

Except with other people's secrets.

Allison got out of my car and walked across the grass toward me with her bag slung over her shoulder, still talking on the phone. "Here she is," she said. She held the phone out to me.

I shook my head.

"Walter," she said. "I told him about the rumors."

I grabbed the phone. "Thank you so much for last night," I exclaimed. "Football is so hard!"

He laughed. "You did a good job. You would be good no matter what. And at half-time the band sounded even better than at homecoming, technically. Did you work on that weird mellophone part in the middle song?"

I knew Walter. I knew there was a but coming. "But?"

"But at homecoming, the show had more . . . I don't know."

"Life."

"Yes! And I think it's Drew. I think the band sounds best when you and Drew direct together."

The third bus parked in front of the band room.

"I didn't make him quit," I reminded Walter. "And I'm not inclined to beg him to come back, after what he did to me. To my family." I did my best Tony Soprano. "Blood is thicker than water. The family sticks together. *Capisce?*"

"I'm glad you still have enough of a sense of humor to do horrible imitations."

"Hey!"

"But listen, Don Corleone. I'm not convinced Drew told the Evil Twins. It doesn't sound like something he'd do."

"How can you say that? You hardly know him. And you call him Patton."

"I just called him that because you liked him. I know him pretty well. I was in Boy Scouts with him for years."

This I couldn't picture. "You were in Boy Scouts?"

"It's not that weird. When you're ten years old and you live in a bus, you do what you can to fit in. And then, by the time you're fifteen, you give up."

The fourth bus parked in front of the band room.

"It doesn't make sense to me, either," I said. "Drew was really mad about losing drum major. But it still doesn't make sense that he'd be out to get me. He doesn't work that way. But who else could have told the twins? Drew is the only person I told."

"Maybe your dad told someone. Does your mom know? Maybe your mom told someone."

"They didn't want Allison's parents to find out. I doubt they told anybody."

"It takes two to tango."

I blinked. "What?"

"Who did your dad have the affair with?"

I shivered in the warm sun. "Some nurse named Lurleen at the hospital. It was over by the time he told my mom and me. I never met her."

The line of boys from the instrument room pitched the last case onto the U-Haul and closed and locked the door.

"A nurse named Lurleen?" Walter asked. "That's the Evil Twins' mother."

On cue, long hair, big boobs, and her sister pulled their car into the parking lot, late. Did this mean we really were the Evil Triplets? "It can't be the same Lurleen," I said calmly. But I pressed my hand to my heart thumping hard in my chest.

"How many nurses named Lurleen do you think work at the hospital?"

"Well, I don't know. And how do *you* know all these people?"

"They rented a trailer in my campground for a few weeks when they were between houses about five years ago, right after their dad left them."

The twins hauled their bags and cooler and flute cases out of their used car and slammed the doors. I glanced over at my own car, which my parents had bought for me brand new when I turned sixteen. Then I glanced back at the twins. One of them was blatantly pointing at me and was probably making some choice comments about me to the other.

It *did* make more sense now, why they would come after me like they had. And it had never occurred to me that Dad had had an affair with someone I knew or the mother of someone I knew, but that made sense too. It *was* a small town.

"They must hate me," I mused. "And now I steal their boyfriend? I'd hate me too!"

"I'm waiting for the other shoe to drop," Walter said.

What was I missing? I went over the whole thing in my mind for the billionth time, then gasped.

"Drew didn't tell them about my dad.

The Evil Twins found out from their mom. Those *bitches*!"

"There you go."

"Oh, Walter, and I was mean to him because I thought he told everybody! And now he's not here! I've been watching the whole time, and he hasn't gotten here yet! And the buses are starting!"

"Go save the day." Walter laughed as he hung up.

Everyone was on the buses but me. And Drew. I dashed across the grass and knocked frantically on the door of the junior bus.

Mr. Rush folded the door open with the lever. He shouted above the noise of the bus engine, "May I help you?"

"We can't leave yet. Drew's not here. I think he may have quit band because of a misunderstanding."

Mr. Rush shook his head. "The two of you aren't communicating."

"Right. Give me time to call him. I bet I can convince him to be drum major again."

"It's too late for that, Sauter. We're on a schedule. We can't wait for Morrow to work out his teen angst."

I moved up one step, into the bus.

"Maybe he's on his way. Maybe he got held up in traffic."

"There's no traffic in this town, Sauter. You're lucky to have a stop sign."

I stomped my boot on the bus step. "I feel desperate!"

"I feel punctual!" Mr. Rush said.

I jumped out of the way as he closed the bus door.

I dashed to the front of the senior bus, stepped on the bumper, and hauled myself up on the hood. I stood there in my uniform jacket, miniskirt, and knee-high boots with my hands on my hips, like Supergirl. Then I pointed through the windshield at the bus driver and commanded, "Turn off the engine!"

The bus driver turned off the engine.

Mr. Scott leaned out the bus door. "Are you allowed to be up there?"

"Yes," I said. "It's a tradition. Before every band contest, the drum major plays hood ornament." I flipped open my phone and dialed Drew's home number.

All the buses had cut their engines now. In the silence I recognized the approaching hum of another motor.

I watched in disbelief as the tractor

turned the corner and Drew parked in front of the bus.

I folded the phone, jumped down from the hood, and fell on my butt. Drew was halfway out of the tractor seat to help me, but I bounded over the tractor tire and up into the cab, into his lap.

Maybe he was still mad at me. Maybe we needed to talk it out and say how we felt. But I was so relieved to see him, I didn't care. I kissed him.

Mmmmmmm. He kissed me back. He didn't seem to be mad.

"Luther called me this morning," he whispered hoarsely. "He said you thought I told the twins about your dad. I didn't. I haven't spoken a word to—" He paused.

"Cacey."

"Right. I haven't spoken a word to Cacey since I broke up with her. Tracey, either." He kissed me.

Mmmmmmm.

"I wouldn't tell your secret," he said. "I wouldn't do that to *anyone*, much less you." He kissed me again.

"Get it, Morrow!" Luther called out the window of the bus behind us.

"Get it, Sauter!" called Allison.

We laughed, then wrapped our arms around each other and hugged hard. It felt so wonderful to finally embrace him again, and rub my cheek against his cheek as I had Sunday afternoon. Or maybe it was just the tractor.

He kissed my jaw, up near my ear.

No, I didn't think it was just the tractor.

"I thought you weren't coming," I breathed.

He said in my ear, "Dad took the car to work, and the truck wouldn't start. I had to get here somehow. It took me forever."

I pulled back to look him in the eye. "Your dad's going to kill you."

"I called him at work and told him what I was doing."

"And he gave you permission?"

"Um, no. But at least I was responsible enough to let him know I was doing it. He'll come to take it home when he gets off the night shift in a few minutes." He gestured toward the line of buses. "It would be best if we left before he got here, if you know what I mean. He's also coming to the contest. If we do well as drum majors, he'll be more likely to forgive me. No pressure."

"Yeah, that's what Mr. Rush said. No

pressure. Ha." Then I realized Drew had said "we"—"if *we* do well as drum majors." I noticed for the first time that he was wearing his drum major uniform. With his Vans.

"I brought my regular band uniform." He kicked a bag in the floorboard. "If you want to be drum major by yourself from now on, I would totally understand, and no hard feelings. I'm sorry I was such an ass before. It took me a little while, you know? I needed twenty-four hours." He looked at his watch. "Well, twenty-one."

"I wasn't mad at you about that. Anyway, not for long. I just thought you'd told the twins about my dad. I didn't know until this morning that my dad had the affair with the twins' mother. They found out and told everyone."

He went very still, and the dark eyes blinked at me. "Your dad and Lurleen?"

I nodded.

His eyes flicked to the bus behind me, where the twins were waiting. "No wonder the twins have been on your case. Maybe they thought you liked me during band camp, and they came on to me and got me to ask them out just to make you mad."

I flushed hot with embarrassment, and put one hand up to my cheek, which I'm sure was bright pink. "That would mean I'm very obvious."

"And that would mean they used me. I feel so cheap!"

We laughed because we were giddy. Then stopped laughing because it wasn't funny.

"Seriously, that's opprobrious." He wrinkled his nose. "Reprehensible."

"Evil, even."

We flinched as the driver of the bus behind us lay on the horn.

"Nnnn," Drew said, waving his hand at the bus driver. He stood me up in the cab so he could slide out of the seat. "Excuse me." He jumped down from the tractor.

"What are you going to do?" I called.

"Yell at a girl."

"Please don't. It doesn't matter now—"

"Nnnn," he said, waving his hand at me.

I ran after him as he strode to the senior bus. He pounded on the door. It opened for him, and he stomped up the steps. I climbed up behind him. I had to hear this.

He pointed to the twin in a seat near the front. "You lay off Virginia."

Everyone on the bus, including the twin, gaped at him in silence for a full five seconds. Then the twin hollered, "I didn't do shit to Virginia."

"Come off it. Everybody knows you're evil. Don't be evil to Virginia. I'm dating Virginia. I'm not dating you, so get over it."

"You never were dating me!" the twin screeched.

He looked at the other twin, who was standing up toward the back of the bus. "You're both capable of the same atrocities. You're genetically identical."

As he stomped down the bus stairs, half the bus clapped. The other half murmured, "Atrocities?"

"Atrocities?" I asked him.

"You burned those SAT words into my brain." He took my hand and swung it as we walked up the street to the freshman bus. "Let's go win a contest."

Twenty-four

"I wouldn't do that to you," Drew whispered for the hundredth time.

We stood close to each other in front of the band, facing the crowded stands of the stadium. As the band was warming up for our performance, Drew had engineered this new way for us to stand at attention while we waited for the signal to do the dip. Instead of keeping a few paces between us across the grass, he stood right behind me, touching me, with his hand curled around my waist.

Because we were at attention and were supposed to stay quiet and still, I resisted the urge to put both my hands over his hand and squeeze to comfort him. He hadn't betrayed me, but he was still horrified that I had ever *thought* he had. I'd been reassuring him all morning and afternoon.

Now that the sun was setting, the announcer droned on and on with the contest scores. All the bands stood at attention on the field. The ones on either side of us squealed with glee when they got high marks, or sagged in defeat otherwise.

We had already done our squealing with glee. Our band had gotten very high scores, and Drew and I had won the award for best drum majors. We had saved Mr. Rush from going back to work at Pizza Hut. For now.

Drew and I had sat together in the stands and watched the performances of most of the bands who'd come before and after us. I was interested in their scores, especially the huge bands that had been in our class. But there were so many scores, and it was a long time to stand still.

I was glad I had Drew's hand on my waist for entertainment. I took a deep breath just to feel his grip tighten and shift when I moved. I felt another phantom limb coming on.

"I can't believe you convinced me to

stand this way," I said quietly, moving my lips as little as possible.

"Why?" He sounded hurt.

"It feels too good. If the judges knew, they'd deduct points."

His chest moved against my back as he tried to swallow his laughter. "There are six games left in the regular season, and I wanted to enjoy them. And speaking of enjoying ourselves, what are you doing tonight?"

I'd been waiting for him to ask me. And I'd been dreading giving him the answer. "The band got such high marks, I figure they'll want to roll Mr. Rush's yard and Oreo his car. It's probably our responsibility as drum majors to make sure everybody chips in for Oreos and toilet paper."

He sighed. "Okay. If the buses get back to the school by eight, do you think we can be out of Mr. Rush's yard by nine?"

"Why? Where are you taking me? Rent 2 Own?"

"Oh, no. Not Rent 2 Own. For you, I've scheduled barn time."

Would this announcer go on *forever*? I wanted me some barn time. I couldn't help giggling in anticipation.

"We've got to stop this," he said, his breath warm against my hair. "The judges really might take our high scores away if they see me talking to my girlfriend at attention."

I tingled at the word "girlfriend." "More likely, your dad will kill you."

"My dad will get over it. Jeez, I drove the tractor to school. And I'm wearing Vans with my uniform."

Squinting against the setting sunlight, I searched the stands for Mr. Morrow. Near him sat my parents, holding hands as usual. I still planned to have a talk with them. The fact that Drew and I hadn't been at fault for spilling their secret didn't make me any less of a troubled teen. Now I was just a troubled teen with a boyfriend.

I was almost looking forward to the talk.

The announcer had reached the most important awards of the night, the best band in each class. He started with the smallest bands and moved up. Then he reached the class we should have been in, if Mr. Rush hadn't been greedy.

"We sounded awesome," I whispered. "We would have won that class."

"Don't talk at attention," Drew said.

I pinched him.

"Ouch. Don't pinch at attention."

I was so sure we hadn't won the highest class that I stopped listening to the drone of the announcer, until the name of our school was called. We had won the award.

What? We had won the award!

I wasn't thinking, but Drew was. We were supposed to do the dip now. He put his hand *there* and his leg *there,* and leaned me back until my head almost touched the grass.

The rest of the band was supposed to stay at attention. They should have waited until we collected the other band officers and marched soberly across the field to claim our own trophy the size of a refrigerator.

But the screaming band swarmed around us. Then past us. The entire band, instruments and all, dashed across the field to the trophy table. Upside down, out the corner of my eye, I noticed that most of them were bareheaded. They left a broad trail of hats on the grass.

Then I looked up into Drew's dark eyes. "I'm glad I'm still drum major," he whispered. "But I'm more glad I'm drum major with you."

The band caught my attention again. They had found Mr. Rush and stood him up against the trophy to measure them. The trophy was slightly taller. About ten boys picked up the trophy over their heads, and another ten picked up Mr. Rush. All of them fell down. Our band was like that.

"Drum major!" they called across the field. "We need a drum major!"

"They can do without us for once," Drew said. He kissed me.

I slid my hands into his hair and kissed him back.

About the Author

Jennifer Echols grew up in Alexander City, Alabama, where she was the first female drum major of her high school marching band. She also played saxophone, trumpet, and drums, and had an extremely unfortunate turn on the oboe. In college, Jennifer majored in music education and composition before she made the switch to English and creative writing. *Major Crush* is her first book.

Dad motions for us to go in my room. "It's best if we have some privacy. This is a very delicate situation."

"A delicate situation?" I repeat, pushing open the door to my bedroom.

Dad looks me square in the eyes and says, "Blaine's going to be staying at our house for an undetermined amount of time."

I raise my eyebrows in surprise. "What do you mean Blaine's going to be staying here?" I ask. "You're kidding, right?"

He shakes his head. "Blaine may be living here for the next couple of months. Possibly until the end of the school year."

My jaw drops. I was expecting him to say *days,* not months. "What do you mean a couple of months?!" I exclaim. "What is he, some long-lost cousin I've never met?"

Dad chuckles. "Funny you should say that. In a way, yes."

A sick feeling comes over me. *Oh my God, I've been flirting with my cousin!* That's seriously gross. "Which side of the family is he on?" I ask, thinking, *I don't recall ever meeting Blaine before.*

"My side," Dad says. "At least, that's what his paperwork will say."

"His paperwork?" I dump the contents of my overnight bag on the bed and begin sorting through the mess.

"Yeah, his new driver's license and school records. The central office should have them ready in a day or two."

I'm totally lost. None of this is making sense. "Why does Blaine need a new driver's license? Did he lose his or something?"

Dad shakes his head. "No, but it's standard fare—it's all part of his FBI cover."

I stare at him, shocked. "Oh my God." I can't think of anything else to say. "As you know, part of my job at the FBI involves keeping tabs on witnesses before they go to trial," Dad continues. "Usually we store them at a safe house or in a hotel to keep them out of harm's way."

I nod. "Right. I understand."

He takes a deep breath. "Kaitlyn, what I'm about to tell you is classified information. You can't breathe a word to anybody. Not even Morgan. Can I trust you?"

Whoa. I've never seen Dad like this before. He looks deadly serious. "Of course you can," I tell him.

My dad stands up and starts pacing the room, swinging his arms back and forth as he walks. As he gets to the far wall, his left foot bumps against my mile-high stack of magazines, sending back issues of *Teen Vogue, CosmoGirl!,* and *Seventeen* toppling over with a crash. Dad keeps right on walking. "Have you ever heard of Harlan Donovan, the Texas oil tycoon?"

I shake my head. "No, but I'm guessing since his last name is Donovan he's related to Blaine. And I'm also guessing that if he's an oil tycoon he's probably a . . ." I pause, gulping, ". . . millionaire."

"Add a few zeroes," Dad says, "and you're about right."

"You don't mean that he's a billionaire!"

"Yes, he is."

He continues with the story. "One of the business deals Harlan Donovan is involved in has been attracting a lot of attention lately. Threats have been made against Harlan and his family—and many of these threats have been targeted at Blaine. We're currently investigating the situation, and we think the people involved may be responsible for strong-arming several other big oil deals. We're trying our hardest to catch them, but at this point in time, we felt it was best to remove Blaine until all of this can be resolved. Once we catch these thugs, or once the business deal is finished—whichever comes first—Blaine will be out of danger, and he can return to the Donovan estate."

"So why is Blaine staying here? Since when does *our house* qualify as a safe house? You've never brought any of the people you're protecting here before."

"The Blaine situation is complicated," Dad says, "and I can't give you the specifics. For now, what I need you to do is not mention Blaine to anyone. *Not a word.*"

I nod my head. "Don't worry. You can count on me. There's just one thing—won't keeping him a secret be kind of tough? I mean, three months is a long time."

"You won't have to keep him a secret for that long," Dad explains. "Once Blaine's new ID and paperwork come in, we'll be able to get to work establishing his cover. I think he's going to be posing as a distant cousin."

I chew on my lower lip. I'm feeling nervous about this, like I won't be able to do it. "So I'm going to have to pretend Blaine is related to me?"

Dad massages his temple, like he's got a headache coming on. "Something like that. I'll give you the full details as soon as I have them. What I need now is a guarantee that you'll keep this, how do you kids say it, *on the down low?*"

"Sure, fine," I say, waving my hand dismissively. "I'll do whatever you need."

"Great! We can talk about this more later," Dad says, heading for the door.

I try to digest everything Dad has told me. It's pretty freaking unbelievable. Dad's never been the type to bring his work home with him. Although, in this case, I don't really mind. A cute boy is welcome in our home anytime as far as I'm concerned. "So what's Blaine going to do while he's here?" I ask, as Dad makes his way to the door. "I mean, won't he be bored out of his mind just sitting around the house all day?"

"Oh, I thought you realized. That's part of why Blaine is staying here," Dad says. "The spring term just started at his old school and it'd be a shame for him to get too far behind in his studies. At first we were planning to get him a private tutor, but things worked out for him to enroll at Copperfield. So, starting in a couple of days, he'll be going to school with you. I trust you'll show Blaine around and make him feel at home? Going to a new school is stressful for anyone, and Blaine has been through a lot lately."

"Of course I will," I tell Dad. And I mean it. I'm going to do whatever I can to make Blaine feel welcome.

"And another thing," Dad says, looking me dead in the eyes. "I don't want to alarm you, but it would probably be a good idea to keep your eyes peeled for anything suspicious while Blaine's in town. We've covered his tracks pretty well, but you can never be completely sure. In some ways, Blaine's life is in your hands."

I feel all the color drain from my swollen face as this sinks in. *His life?* Good grief, I can barely take care of my *own* life. Just last month I sprained my ankle while trying to rearrange my closet. I must look pretty panicked, because Dad immediately adds, "That probably didn't come out right. What I meant was, I'd like for you to keep an eye on Blaine, just make sure nobody treats him oddly or takes an unnatural interest in him. And if anybody calls here asking for him, you let me know *immediately*. If that happens, we've got an emergency situation on our hands."

"Wow," I say. "This is totally bizarre."

Dad smiles reassuringly as he walks out the door. "Just think of yourself as a junior undercover agent."

At those words, a chill runs down my spine. *A junior undercover agent.* A spy. I feel electrified, energized. Almost like a mini Sydney Bristow. Except with shorter legs. And frizzier hair.

Seven Sins.

Seven Books.

Seven Teens . . .

. . . all determined to get what they
want, when they want it. No matter
the cost, or the drama.

LUST   ENVY   **PRIDE**   WRATH
SLOTH   GLUTTONY   GREED

SEVEN DEADLY SINS
BY ROBIN WASSERMAN

Commit the third sin
in this juicy series!

From Simon Pulse
Published by Simon & Schuster

truth or dare

By the bestselling author of the Mates, Dates series,

Cathy Hopkins

Meet Cat, Becca, Squidge, Mac, and Lia. These girls and guys are totally tight—and totally obsessed with the game of truth or dare . . . even when it reveals too much!

Every book is a different dare . . . and a fun new adventure.

Read them all:

From Simon Pulse
Published by Simon & Schuster